EASY MEAT

Rachel Trezise

PARTHIAN

'*Easy Meat* is a poignant and vivid depiction of life in the South Wales Valleys for Caleb, a typical Valleys boy whose life is spiralling out of control… a sensitive portrayal of people as people – full, complex and multifaceted – whose every choice is shaped by the conflicting experiences and identities that inform who we are."

Polly Winn, founder of the Cardiff Feminist Book Club,
the welsh agenda

RACHEL TREZISE

Parthian, Cardigan SA43 1ED
www.parthianbooks.com
© Rachel Trezise 2021
ISBN print: 9781914595875
ISBN ebook: 978-1-913640-40-8
Editor: Gwen Davies
Cover Design: Marc Jennings
Typeset by Elaine Sharples
Printed by 4edge Limited
Published with the financial support of the Books Council of Wales
British Library Cataloguing in Publication Data
A cataloguing record for this book is available from the British Library.

Rachel Trezise's debut novel *In and Out of the Goldfish Bowl* won a place on the Orange Futures List in 2002. In 2006 her first short fiction collection *Fresh Apples* won the Dylan Thomas Prize. Her second short fiction collection *Cosmic Latte* won the Edge Hill Prize Readers Award in 2014. Her first play *Tonypandemonium* was produced by National Theatre Wales in 2013 and won the Theatre Critics of Wales Award for best production. Her second play for National Theatre Wales, *We're Still Here*, premiered in September 2017. Her latest play, *Cotton Fingers*, also for National Theatre Wales, has recently toured Ireland and Wales. At the Edinburgh Fringe Festival 2019 it was chosen by The Stage as one of the best shows in the festival and received a Summerhall Lustrum Award. Her debut novel has recently been reissued in the Library of Wales series.

Fiction
In and Out of the Goldfish Bowl
Fresh Apples
Sixteen Shades of Crazy
Cosmic Latte
Easy Meat

Drama
Tonypandemonium
We're Still Here
Cotton Fingers

Non-fiction
Dial M for Merthyr

All over people changing their votes
Along with their overcoats
If Adolf Hitler flew in today
They'd send a limousine anyway

– Joe Strummer,
'(White Man) In Hammersmith Palais'

The sound of gunshots came and went, barely penetrating Caleb's sleep. Steadily he began to register them, and – beneath them – heavy breathing, menacing but familiar. A stench of weed had saturated the tiny bedroom, he could taste it behind his nostrils and feel it coating his tongue. He kept his eyes closed against the artificial light until he heard an urgent clatter of plastic fracturing. He opened his eyes to his younger brother sprawled on the bed opposite, a video game frozen on the TV screen. There was only one bed and his brother was sleeping in it for the month – he'd been lucky enough to call Prince's opiate overdose in their ongoing game of celebrity death pool. It was a bumper year, David Bowie, Muhammad Ali and the rapper from A Tribe Called Quest, all gone. 'Sorry bro,' Mason said. 'I can't get the head off the last mannequin in Nuketown. It's gripping my balls.' The Xbox controller was on the floor against the skirting board, batteries spilled on the carpet.

Caleb could see through the Spiderman curtains that it was light outside. His phone was plugged in the charger next to Mason's bed. 'What's the time then, butt?' he asked his brother.

'Ten to five.' Mason took a lit spliff from the dirty mug on the floor next to the bed and sucked greedily on it. 'The fuck is that?' Caleb asked, tasting the cannabis anew. 'Smells rank.' He raised himself onto his elbows, the metal springs hard in the thin mattress of the rolled-out bed settee.

'Special Kush. Chill as anything. Have a go.' Mason handed the spliff down to Caleb then produced a can of Lynx Apollo from under his pillow and sprayed it into the air. Before Caleb knew what he was doing the roach of the zoot was between his lips, the bitter smoke burning the back of his throat. 'Shit, Mase!' he said, remembering he'd given up smoking six weeks ago. 'You

1

know I'm trying to stay on the straight and narrow.' He handed the spliff back to his brother. He tried to cough the weed out of his lungs.

Mason laughed. 'I ain't your keeper am I?'

'Yes!' Caleb said. 'We're supposed to look out for each other.'

'You are, bro. You're the oldest.' He took a hit off the spliff. 'Guess what happened to me last night anyway,' he said. 'Wait 'til I tell you.' Caleb hoiked his head at his brother as if to say, '*Go on.*' His alarm hadn't gone off yet. He still had time. 'That barmaid in the Centaur,' Mason said. 'The ginger one with the rack. She only asked me to fuck 'er, didn't she? "When're you gonna fuck me, Mase?" she says when she's giving me my three quid change. Fuckin' gob-struck, bro.'

'That's why you're here playing Call of Duty.'

'I wouldn't do that to Brandy, would I?'

'I don't know. It's not like Brandy's your real girlfriend, is it? She's a million miles away, on the other side of the globe.'

'Globe?' Mason said. 'As if.'

'She's eating corn dogs in Central Park.'

'Bro, I told you she lives where Breaking Bad is set. It's the desert not New York.'

Caleb broke into the chorus of a song he'd heard the old man listening to in the car: '*Hot dog! Jumping Frog!*'

'What do you know about real girlfriends anyway?' Mason said, cutting him off.

Caleb threw the duvet off his chest, the cool morning air hitting his skin like a slap. He sat up, settee springs creaking. 'What were you doing up the Centaur on a Wednesday anyway? I thought you were skint.' He took an old polo shirt from the pile of clothes draped over the arm of the settee and pulled it over his head.

'Had to see Kinsey, didn't I? He owed me a tenner for that

2

eighth of soap we bought for bank holiday. Kinsey practically lives in the Centaur.'

'Bank holiday? What's so special about a bank holiday when you're unemployed, Mase?'

'Fuckin' hell bro! Wind your neck in. It's none of your business where I go on a Wednesday or on bank holiday or anything.'

'You're either half-baked or you're out on the piss. You're supposed to be looking for a job.'

Mason shout-whispered at Caleb: 'There ain't any jobs to find, Cal. I'm doing all the work the agency will give me. That's what a zero-hours contract is; zero fucking hours! Not that it's anything to do with you. You ain't my boss, butt!'

Caleb zipped the fly of his jeans and reached towards his brother's bedside for his mobile phone. 'Man up, Mase,' he said, unclipping the jack. 'Unless you want a pasting. I'm sick of being the only responsible one here.'

'Chillax, bro,' Mason said. 'Before you get an ulcer or summin. You've been like a coiled spring ever since that fucking court case.'

Caleb dropped his phone and grabbed the neck of his brother's hoodie, lifting him an inch off the bed. 'Don't talk to me like that, you little shit,' he said glaring straight into Mason's bloodshot eyes. 'I'm the one who pays the mortgage here.' With that the alarm on his phone started up, a high-pitched whir like a siren at a nuclear plant. He let go of his brother to retrieve it, rushing to cut the alarm before it woke his parents in the room next door. He slid it into the arse pocket of his jeans and turned to go.

'Chuck me that over,' Mason said, gesturing at the Xbox controller on the floor.

Caleb sighed as he stooped to recover it, then side armed it back to his brother like a pebble into a river, Mason flinching as it landed in his lap, the batteries left where they were. 'Clean this shit up,' he said, nodding at the clothes and video game cases piled at the base of Mason's bed. 'The least you can do is keep the place tidy.'

'*You* clean it,' Mason said, because he had to have the last word. 'It's *your* fucking house.'

Caleb slammed the door and stood for a microsecond on the landing gritting his teeth, full of an aggressive energy he didn't know where to put. He had to find a way to harness it, use it for his training when he got back after work. He counted to five in his head, took a breath, then began down the stairs.

Three big bunches of flowers were propped in two vases and a pint glass of water on the worktop in the little kitchenette, roses and lilies and other things Caleb didn't know the names of. 'Fuck knows,' he said breathing in their green scent, failing to guess where they'd come from or where they were meant to go.

He could see a couple of handfuls of wheat bran left in one of the tupperware containers stacked on the table so he took a bowl from the cupboard and the milk from the fridge. Once he'd poured it all out he stood staring out of the window, spooning the tasteless cereal into his mouth, chewing it robotically before swallowing it down. It needed something sweet. Blueberries were an antioxidant, one of the superfoods listed in his guide to the optimal nutrient diet. But he wasn't the one who did the shopping. His mother never bought any fruit anymore. He felt marginally woozy from being up too early, an odd sensation that reminded him of family holidays in Tenerife; setting the alarm to drive to Bristol in the middle of the night, drinking Guinness with Mason and the old man in the airport bar at five a.m. Eating dinner at the Empire Steak House on the Avenida de Las Américas six hours later. All that felt like a lifetime ago. He hadn't been on an aeroplane for four or five years.

He put the cereal bowl down on the draining board and stared at his reflection in the window, the fridge whirring across the lonely calm. Behind the outline of himself he could see the mound of earth his father had made in the garden trying to dig out by its roots the clump of Japanese knotweed growing against the boundary wall. He wondered what Savannah was doing now; if she was up yet, eating her own breakfast. She was the one with the restraining order, but it was Caleb who couldn't get her out of his mind, not even after all this time. He tried to push the thought away before it began to sting. It was ten past five by the grease-splattered wall clock. He was leaving early for once. He flicked the kitchenette light out and traipsed through the murky living room, grabbing his car keys from the wooden serving bowl on the cupboard in the hallway, ignoring the heap of letters addressed to him mounted up next to it.

There was a thin layer of dew on the roofs of the cars parked all the way along the street. The front of Fat Gary's Nissan was parked on the pavement, arse end sticking out into the road. Caleb walked around it to his own, a third-hand Ford Puma he'd bought with the money left from the sale of his cherished Volkswagen Transporter. A stupid hairdresser's runaround parked flush against the curb. The clutch of grey heron chicks in the tree behind the old garages brayed like a bunch of hungry donkeys as he opened the car door. The dramatic orchestral prelude to The Streets' *A Grand Don't Come for Free* heaved from the stereo speakers as he switched the engine on. He reached for the volume, turning it down a pinch as he manoeuvred out of his space between the Nissan and a white Transit van. A view of the whole width of the valley unfurled in the windscreen as he turned the corner out of the street, the glacial cirques of the Pontio mountain, its lower slopes blackened by grass fires. He drove over the railway bridge into Tregele, going through the red light on Pegasus Square because it rarely changed at that time in the morning. The council bin lorry tailed him up the high street.

He eased his foot onto the brake slowing the car when he saw the handwritten sign stuck in his father's old carpet shop window: 'Opening Soon. Amazing Glazing.' 'The fuck?' he said to himself. The bin lorry beeped its horn. Caleb had brought the traffic behind him to a standstill. 'Amazing Glazing?' he said to himself as he reluctantly shifted into gear and set off towards Trehumphrey, top lip stretched into a sneer. It would have to be a window installation business with a name like that. But a window place wouldn't last long in Rhosybol, not with Warmaglaze in Penyrenglyn and Zodiac Windows in Caemawr. Not to mention South Wales Windows at the other end of the valley. The shop had been empty since the bank had repossessed it in February.

His father had owned it outright. Then carpet went out of fashion. There was this DIY programme that came on the telly, interior designers reimagining terraced houses with cheap fibreboards made to look like real wood instead of traditional patterned Wilton. His father thought it was a fad that'd peter out within a few years. 'There's a reason we're called *Just* Carpets,' he'd say pointing his finger at the shop sign hanging up outside. 'We don't do rugs or laminate or tiles. We do carpet.' He had a motto he'd learned on his business course: 'Invest in what you know – that way it's either all your credit or all your fault.' So instead of branching out they'd decided to remortgage. Austerity hit the valleys hard. Caleb remembered reading a story in the *Rhosybol Herald* about the use of a Food Bank in Penllechau quadrupling overnight. Eventually his old man had lost the shop and the Ninian Close villa his parents had put down as security. They had to move in with him. His brother came with them. Caleb's plan was to get the shop back. If he could source laminate for the same price B&Q got it the business would run itself. Stack it high, sell it cheap. All he had to do was keep paying the mortgage on his house in Iscoed Street. That way he had something to secure a loan against when he'd finally saved enough for the deposit.

It was twenty past five when he rounded the first crook of the Bryn mountain road. Sunrays lit the garlands of gold tinsel strung on the fir tree in the Pen Foel picnic area. Late last year someone had decorated it with Christmas baubles and glitter. It was almost the end of June now, the trimmings had stuck fast. They must have used Gorilla Glue. Caleb remembered when he was little, the last watchman to work in the watchman's hut had decorated the craggy parts of the lower mountain with strange flowers he fashioned out of plastic grocery bags. The council had already secured the falling rocks with wire mesh so he didn't have much work keeping the road clear. He kept showing up everyday anyway, working on his art project instead. Then he died and the flowers washed away. Sad all around, Caleb thought. The sun was picking up strength, the landscape coming to life the way a polaroid develops: ferns and clusters of heather, yellow grass peppered with clods of brown reeds. The wind turbines dotted along the ridge stood motionless, the tips of their huge white blades jutting above the mountain's summit. At the top he could see the rest of the road stretched below, an elongated hairpin like a colossal section of Scalextric and the oily-looking reservoir below. The sun gleamed on the reflective paint of the crash barrier overlooking the old colliery. Apparently there were plans to build Europe's fastest zip line, and thrill seekers from all over the world were going to travel to fly down the length of the Bryn on a pulley at a hundred miles an hour. His mother loved this idea. 'Rhosybol could be a tourist goldmine,' she always said, 'what with all the mountains and lakes. Why couldn't it? It's beautiful.' As he neared the end of the road he saw a warning sign set up in the middle of the road. He slowed as he approached it, then came to a full stop, brake pedal pushed to the floor. White words on a blue background: Police. Accident.

Blue lights were pulsing beyond the roundabout, but Caleb couldn't see the problem. He waited a few seconds, Mike Skinner going on about a girl in the queue at McDonald's who was fit but knew it, guitar chugging. He reversed and slowly steered around the sign, nudging the car ahead a few inches at a time, then stopped. He waited another second then released his seatbelt. The magpies quarrelling in the scrub on the embankment flew off when he slammed the car door. He tramped to the island in the middle of the roundabout where he saw that the lights were coming from a police car parked on the verge of the main road. Behind it a blue car was smashed against the stilts of the Hebron signpost. There was a body slumped out of the driver's window, tangled into an unnatural shape. A policewoman sitting in the cop car gestured at Caleb to move back. He drifted towards the edge of the island and lingered at the kerb while the woman got out of the car and walked towards him. 'There's nothing I can do on my own,' she said. 'The paramedics are on their way.' She looked down at her feet.

'Is he dead?' Caleb said. He'd never seen a dead body before. His mother and father and brother had been at the hospital when Gankey Jenkins died but Caleb was in the car park outside, bickering with Savannah. 'I'm not sure.' The brim of the policewoman's helmet cast a shadow over her heavily made-up face. 'The paramedics should be here soon.' She pointed at the bonnet of his car. 'You'll need to turn around. This road is closed now.'

'But I'm on my way to work. I need to be in Derwen by six.'

'I'm sorry. I can't let you through.'

'You're joking,' Caleb said. He had to get to work.

'Absolutely not. You can see this is the scene of a serious accident.' She pressed her brogues into the tarmac, her height gaining a temporary inch.

Morris'd do his nut if Caleb wasn't there in time to boot up. 'Going through Pant'll add an hour to my journey. There wasn't a sign in Trehumphrey. I wouldn't have come all the way over the mountain if there'd been a sign over there, would I?'

'I've only just responded. An officer's on his way with the traffic board for the Trehumphrey entrance.' She looked sharply away.

'There's no harm in letting me through,' Caleb said as cordially as he could.

'Sir!' the policewoman barked at him. 'You need to turn around now.'

Caleb raised his eyebrows, peering at her with puppy dog eyes. She stared right back into his pupils like an optician searching for a defect. Were his eyes dilated? Could she tell he'd smoked a bit of spliff? 'Alright,' he said, turning away from her. It was useless to try to appeal to the sense of humanity in a cog in the corporate machine. He headed back to the car. 'Bollocks!' he said to himself as he got inside. He turned the engine on, the stereo starting up with the shrill key of a new song. He turned the car around, the policewoman still watching him from the island in the middle of the roundabout. She shrunk to a stick figure in the rear-view mirror as he sped back up the straight towards the mountain. A car pulled around the curve below the reservoir, heading down into the valley. He flashed his lights as it approached. The driver flashed back at him, mistaking his signal for a warning about a speed camera or a roaming flock of sheep.

Two plods were crouched at the edge of the cattle grid in Trehumphrey, erecting the road sign the policewoman at the accident had promised, their bright yellow hi-vis jackets dazzling against the mossy green of the ferns on the ridge. A delivery lorry was unloading a pallet of shrink-wrapped paint in front of the decorating shop at the top of the high street. Sanjoy was lifting the shutters on the newsagent next door to the laundrette. The lights were on in the old man's carpet shop, two glowing orbs shining through the brown paper lining the windows. 'Amazing Glazing,' he said reading the sign again.

Dai Fib was picking a fag butt out of the ashtray in front of the beauticians, his long white hair slicked back. Caleb had been in the library with the two Joshes one afternoon, bunking off maths when Dai Fib, who practically lived in an armchair in the large-print section, told them he'd grown the biggest pumpkin known to man. 'I made the Guinness Book of Records, didn't I? 1989. Look it up.'

'Bullshit,' Rod Eynon said from the computer suite. 'You've been sleeping in the bunker under the rugby pitch since 1970. Where the hell would you have grown a pumpkin?' Dai Fib got up in a huff and marched out of the large-print section.

'Why does he do that?' Josh Webber asked Eynon. 'He told us last week he used to wrestle bears in Russia. He's only 5′ 4″.'

'No idea,' Eynon said. 'Sure to be he loves a tall tale. Harmless enough otherwise. Wouldn't hurt a fly nevermind a bear.'

As Caleb drove out of Tregele into Trefecca, he recognised the heady odour of the petrol tank churning dregs. He'd *had* enough fuel to get him over the Bryn, and his plan had been to fill up in the PriceCo garage on Derwen Uchaf; it was only a quid to the litre over there. 'Bollocks to it,' he said as he finally acknowledged the fuel gauge needle dipping below the big E. When the Gwynfa Road traffic lights turned green he indicated right into the exorbitant Texaco.

He pulled up at the pump and got out of the car. The train was pulling into Trefecca railway station with a screech as he hooked the petrol nozzle into the tank. He pressed lightly on the trigger, watching over his shoulder as the numbers whizzed around on the electronic screen. He lifted his forefinger off the handle the zeptosecond the digits turned to 19.99 ensuring the total came to a flat twenty quid.

He walked across the forecourt into the garage shop, the door sensor chiming above him. He picked up two KitKat Chunkys from the shelf of chocolates while he waited for the cashier to serve the motorcyclist ahead of him. 'Yes, mate?' the cashier said when the motorcyclist moved off, helmet cradled in his arm. Caleb put his chocolate bars down on the counter and the cashier rang them up with the fuel, the total appearing in green on the till's VDU: £21.22. Caleb handed his debit card over. When the rasp of the printer didn't start he knew it had been declined. It was Thursday morning. He didn't get paid until midnight. 'Try this,' he said reluctantly sliding his credit card out of his wallet. Without looking at the cashier he handed it over with an irritable sigh, sick to his back teeth of being on his arse. By the time he'd paid the mortgage and the minimum payment on the card, then shelled out for the fuel he needed to get to work and back, he had nothing left for anything nice. But every month he got closer to the credit limit, then the same vicious cycle repeated itself all over again. Whatever Morris threw at him he caught; a freeze on his wages, overtime on demand, the ban on discussing his salary with his co-workers. What else was he going to do? He needed that precious monthly deposit, piddling as it was, to pay the bills and safeguard his credit score. The machine had made it so that nobody could function in the world without a respectable credit score. It had to be high enough to make you look credit worthy but low enough to warrant lending in the first place. A bad credit rating was worse than being in jail. Two late payments in a row and the whole thing went kaboosh. He was trying to walk on a tightrope without bending his knees.

The cashier turned the card machine around to face Caleb. He entered the pin number which was Savvy's birthdate. He didn't want to change it because he'd learned it by heart.

'All done,' the cashier said as the payment went through.

Caleb almost smiled in relief. 'Cheers pal,' he said, scooping up his KitKats. He strode out of the shop, the door sensor clanging as he happily heaved it open, free to ride again.

Back on the road, Caleb went easy until he'd passed the speed camera on the green in front of Dunvant Rise. Then he shifted into third. There was a For Sale sign on the bungalow at the top of Red Rose Hill. It was one of the last houses they'd worked in before the business went tits-up in a ditch. Caleb remembered it because his mother had had to order the hand-woven carpet from a specialist wholesaler in Somerset; champagne soft pile. Demand for that kind of quality was rare. On the first morning on the job, Mason had rifled through the daughter's underwear drawer and found a vibrator made out of glittery purple plastic. He brought it down to the kitchen-diner where Caleb was working on a gripper. 'Look at this, bro! Bro! Look at this.' Wormy purple slivers were raised along the length of it. Caleb remembered being offended by it, mentally comparing it to his own smooth-

12

as-stone cock. He laughed uneasily when Mason took the pepper grinder from beside the hob and tipped some of the grains out onto the vibrator. 'That'll confuse her, the dirty bitch.'

They were still working there when the girl got back from college in the afternoon and made them little cups of cappuccino. 'It's got fifteen different grind settings,' she'd said. 'You can have the beans as fine or as coarse as you want.' The old man who'd only ever drunk instant, listened as if she was interpreting Pythagoras' Theorem. 'Wicked,' Mason said, faux-enthusiastic. 'I love grinding, I do.' The girl rolled her eyes at that but by the time they'd finished the job the next day, Mason had got her mobile number. Before he'd got completely strung out on conspiracy theories, his brother had been a cocky little bastard, out to seduce the knickers off the world. Women *love* a cocky bastard.

It was six thirty-five by the clock on the dash when he hit the tailbacks on the Rhosybol Road into Pantyfynnon, traffic queued from the chapel in Hensoltown all the way down to the viaduct. He wasn't going anywhere so he let out a blue Subaru jeep from Grongaer Terrace. The driver gave him a thumbs-up out of his window, gargantuan bicep flexed. Caleb unconsciously tucked his hand behind his arm and pressed his fingers into his flesh to make his own bicep look bigger. He was still half an hour away from Derwen. He thought about phoning in, but he didn't want to hear Morris' voice and he quickly dismissed the idea. He reached into the recess of his door and grabbed one of the KitKats. He split the foil wrapper open with his teeth and gnawed at the edge of the bar where the chocolate was thickest, the biscuit underneath crumbling to a sugary dust, plugging the fissures between his molars. It was the most beautiful thing he'd ever eaten; sweet and crunchy and gooey. In a few moments, the whole thing was gone. He dropped the crumpled wrapper into the cupholder in the gearbox and reached into the recess for the second KitKat. Somewhere in the back of his mind was the vague notion that he was doing something wrong but he couldn't stop himself now. He was halfway through the second bar, thinking about writing an email to Nestlé to suggest they create a KitKat made up of four chunky bars, like a regular four-finger KitKat but big and fat and extra delicious, his taste buds tingling, a little orgasm going off in the insides of his cheeks, when he realised something: he had the munchies. He'd been stoned, and now that it was wearing off, he was craving carbohydrates. He was supposed to be on this optimal nutrient diet; protein and complex carbs only. The car behind him beeped abruptly. The traffic in front of him was creeping towards the dual carriageway. He dropped his half-eaten KitKat into the cup holder and edged the car on.

'Dry Your Eyes' came on the stereo, the acoustic guitar sad and slow. He nodded his head to the stark sixteenth-note beat. It was six forty-five by the clock on the dash as he took the second exit on the roundabout to Maesygwaith. He tried to swallow the last of the melted KitKat left in his mouth, only to find the muscles at the apex of his throat taut and swollen. These song lyrics were getting to him. He reached over to the glovebox and pulled out a new CD: *White Men are Black Men Too*. He'd bought it last year, lured by the name of the group, 'Young Fathers' and only listened to it a couple of times. He hit eject, the Streets disc expelled from the stereo like a silver tongue out of a robot's mouth. He threw it onto the passenger seat and balanced the Young Fathers case on his kneecap, struggling to remove the disc while still holding the steering wheel with his left hand. When he'd got it out, he slipped it into the stereo, the first track starting with a mad synthesiser riff, buzzing like a mosquito crossed with a chainsaw. He slid into the right lane to overtake a haulage truck carrying a mini digger, then sidled back to the left, foot pressed on the accelerator, maintaining a steady 70 mph. The chorus to the song launched like a rocket, a pulsating keyboard lick underneath it, setting Caleb's nerves on edge. The song was about running away from something.

It must have been a sign. He knew he had to hit the pavement when he got back that evening. He'd promised himself he'd start running last Thursday but by the time he'd got back from his shift he was worn out. His mother had wanted a lift to the M&S in Temple Green to get a birthday present for Council Christine, then his old man wanted taxiing home from band practice down the Fickle Dragon. Caleb's evening had leaked away like sand in an hourglass. He was on track with his cycling. Every Sunday he rode over the Pontio to the Gwaun Valley, pushing himself until he lost all feeling in his limbs, delirious with hunger and fatigue. He wasn't too far behind with the swimming. He swam in the pool at Maesygwaith Leisure Centre after work on a Friday night. It was practically empty then, everyone with a life gone to Nando's or the 'Spoons in town for drinks. It was the running that was the real obstacle, the one thing he couldn't seem to motivate himself to do. He only had three months left to train. The Swansea triathlon was on September 24th, a 950-metre swim course off Limeslade Bay followed by a fifty-six-mile bike route around the Gower then four laps of the six-mile-long Mumbles Road.

It was six years since Caleb had won the Talachddu triathlon on his 21st birthday, and five years since he'd finished the Ironman in ten hours and seven seconds, winning the 18–24 category, ranking fifth overall. It'd made him a *celebutant* for a couple of weeks, interviewed on BT Sport and BBC Wales. He'd made the front cover of the *Rhosybol Herald* and the sports pages of the *South Wales Echo*. Men he'd never met before bought him pints in the Centaur. Women in PriceCo flushed pink when he passed them in the cereal aisle. Then he'd been invited by a model scout to audition for a reality TV programme called *Made in Wales* that Channel 4 were making, about a group of young people from the South Wales Valleys moving to a luxury Cardiff Bay apartment to live out their modelling dreams with the help of a couple of mentors; a fitness instructor who'd worked with Cardiff City Football Club and a former glamour model for *Nuts*. As a result, he'd been a cast member on the 2012 series, with seven other twenty-somethings from every *Abercwmnowhere* in post-industrial south Wales, bodybuilders with the IQ of crayons, ballooned on steroids, and Pinot Grigio-soaked Beyoncé wannabes. It was TV designed for rubberneckers who thought the salad always looked greener in someone else's kebab. His old man had been mortified but Caleb didn't mind getting paid to go to parties at Motion and Thekla every other night of the week. One time, a seventeen-year-old girl travelled alone from Glasgow to Tregele to get his autograph, having tracked him down to Just Carpets. Caleb's mother, dumbfounded by the girl's tenacity, made her eat a chip butty from Greaser's and phone home to Scotland to let her parents know she was safe.

Channel 4 didn't renew his contract for the second series; obviously, he hadn't appeared stupid enough to make the show's fallacious storylines look believable. It meant he had more time to spend at the health suite. But when his old man lost the shop, he stopped driving to Temple Green to go to the gym. Instead he started running up the old Cwmyoy railway line, weights strapped to his ankles. He'd do it in the driving rain, the horses in the stables flanking the river watching him quizzically. That was until one night late last year, when he was sprinting a loop around the sunken mine and one of the teenage boys huddled below the drystone wall called out to him: 'Jenks boy! Saw you in the paper!' The other kids in the pack hooting like pantomime villains, the glowing tip of their spliff zig-zagging around in the dark. 'Pussywhipped by a psycho!' one of them said.

Caleb stopped running. 'The fuck?' he shouted back, pulse going ten to the dozen. That wasn't the kind of attention he was used to; he used to be the local hero.

'Savannah Sayer mugged you off. We all read about it.'

That was it. The cat was out of the bag. Caleb stopped going out in public, stopped running altogether. At least on the bike, he had his headwear to hide behind. He could go swimming in the pool in the other valley. He'd begun spending more and more time in the bedroom, smoking weed with his little brother. He'd had no interest in cannabis before then, but that night when he'd got back Mason offered him half a zoot, just a little bit of resin mixed with the tobacco from a single Lambert & Butler. He'd fallen back onto the broken bed settee as if it was the emperor-sized mattress from his room in the Princesa Resort in Lanzarote, and watched hundreds of patches of intense colour dance on the lens of his mind's eye like one of those kaleidoscope things he'd looked into as a kid. The bedroom was vibrating. He couldn't move. He was fixed to the spot. Mason was watching one of his YouTube videos about the secret tunnels under Denver airport, or footage of ISIS beheading one of their hostages, or the clip of the mortuary worker laying down raw rashers of bacon on a dead Muslim's body; he couldn't remember.

All Caleb could do was contemplate the spots of neon red going around in his head. It was as if the YouTube video, which couldn't have been much longer than seven minutes, actually went on for seven hours, like the world was standing still, like Caleb could dip in and out of reality while the rest of the planet paused just for him. But now his muscles were turning to fat. His body was slowing down. The last thing he wanted was to end up like the Penllechau snooker player, Leon Prosser. In 1999, Prosser had been the world number one, the Prince of Wales, Rhosybol Valley's pride and joy. Now he was an alkie who sat at the bar in Penrhiwtyn Workies, stinking of his own piss. Banned from the Masters Tournament for twelve months after testing positive for drugs, he'd sold off his cues one by one for gram baggies of coke. Then he'd taken a job as a roofer but fell off the first one he'd tried to do, smashing his right humorous into a thousand little bits – the butt of jokes about funny bones the world over.

Caleb *had* to get back to the point in his life when he'd been winning. It wasn't too late. All he had to do was get up off his weed-smoking arse and start running. If he could just cross that finish line in Swansea, he knew everything would fall into place. If he couldn't, he knew the few things he had going for himself were going to go to pieces.

As he hit the roundabout at Derwen Uchaf, Caleb's ears popped. A thick belt of mist orbited the business park like a ring around Saturn. This part of Maesygwaith was so high above sea level, even in midsummer it could take until late afternoon to properly clear. He smiled as he passed the signpost for Fochrhiw. 'Yeh, Fuck you.' He drove up the hill towards the warehouse and around the staff car park a few times in search of a space before settling for the kerb behind the council rubbish tip. Everyone on dayshift had already arrived because he was more than an hour late. He blindly rifled through the glove box until he felt the slick plastic coating his staff swipe card. As soon as he'd opened the car door he heard the low warbling from the unloading area on the other side of the site. He grabbed his rucksack from the backseat and set off, darting toward the entry gate. He kept his nostrils closed, postponing the advent of the putrid stench of death. But the moment he passed through the metal grille he could taste as well as smell the slaughterhouse, raw and elemental, buoyed at the back of his throat like a hot bubble of blood.

Caleb trekked toward the corrugated warehouse, the CCTV cameras, fixed along the top of the building, tilting to follow him. He flashed his pass at the square-headed security guard minding the main door. Inside, he headed along the bare white corridor, after ten metres coming to the empty locker room. From his cabinet on the middle tier he grabbed a fresh overall and his size eleven boots, the white rubber soles stained blue from the chemical wash. He got into the smock, twisting this way and that until the heavy cotton settled on his shoulders. He stepped into the wellies and stretched the elastic hem of his hairnet down over his earlobes. He grabbed his white hard hat before throwing his trainers, rucksack and keys into his locker.

He could hear the din of the saw blades as he marched to the shop floor, rubber boots squeaking on the vinyl, temperature rapidly dropping. He stopped at the sink beside the strip curtain and thumped the soap dispenser, a glob of pink mixture spluttering into the bowl of his hand. He rubbed the soap into his palms then rinsed it off in the steaming water. He snatched a new pair of latex gloves from the box on the wall and burst through the PVC strips, eyes blinking against the blazing white lights.

Morris was stooped over the edge of the cutting table, talking to the girl at the end of the line, his red supervisor's hat distinctive among the workers' white bump caps. 'Absolute scenes!' he was saying, dramatically throwing his arms around, a grin slapped across his boulder of a chin. 'That's what you get when you go on your holibobs with the famalam!' Then, as if sensing Caleb's presence, he turned away from the woman and straightened up. 'Jenkins!' he said, scooting across the floor towards him. Caleb could smell his halitosis the centisecond he arrived: 'Where've you been until now?'

Caleb had to think about it; the car crash in Hebron felt like a little lifetime ago, he'd been to so many other places since then. 'Accident,' he blurted as the memory came to him. 'Just off the Bryn road. Car crushed up like a coke can. Body hanging out of it.' He felt an impromptu rush of sympathy for the cadaver he'd seen suspended from the window like a trapeze artist. 'The copper on duty wouldn't let me pass. She made me turn around, come all the way back up through Pantyfynnon.'

'Accident?' Morris said. 'The first I've heard about it.'

Caleb looked down the line of workers on the cutting table. They were all local to the Maesygwaith area. Most of them lived on the Cefn Ifor housing estate two miles away. 'I know I should have phoned in, but I didn't get a chance.' Caleb shrugged. 'I floored it all the way up the A470.'

'What caused the accident?' Morris said, a cunning tone to his voice like he was trying to catch Caleb out. 'It was over before I got there. All I saw was the car crumpled up against the signpost and that feller, dead as a dodo. I left the house earlier than usual.'

'Hmm,' Morris said. He narrowed his raisin-black eyes.

Caleb crossed his arms and kicked at the thin sheet of bloody water, pooled on the concrete floor. From a lopsided angle, Morris stared at Caleb's face until he looked back at him. 'We can't afford anymore mishaps like this going forward,' he said with his slight lisp, the gel caked on the ends of his silt-coloured hair drying under the bright factory lights. 'We're up against it today. We're inundated.'

Caleb dutifully nodded.

'You'll have to make your hour up by the end of the day today.'

'Fine.' He looked past Morris to his space on the butcher's rail but stayed where he was, waiting for the supervisor to dismiss him. Caleb's philosophy was to get through the working day as quickly and quietly as he could. Head down, arse up. Drawing unnecessary attention to yourself in work only ever brought trouble. 'Go on then,' Morris said, now that there was nothing left to say. He clapped his hands at Caleb. 'Winner, winner, chicken dinner.'

Caleb stomped off towards the rail, sniggering at the expression as he went. Morris was full of twee terminology that seemed to boil Caleb's piss. He was a metre away from his place on the rail when he realised the supervisor was still behind him, hands propped on his hips like an angry woman. He'd followed him into the primary butchering area. 'What was that?' he said to Caleb.

'What was what?'

'You said something under your breath. What did you say?'

'Nothing!' Caleb said, dazed at Morris' nitpicking. 'I coughed. I cleared my throat.'

Morris peered down the line of bump-capped workers on the cutting table, filleting knives taut in their hands, a blotchy red rash developing on the pallid skin of his neck. 'Do you think I won't sack you *like that*?' he said, clicking his fat fingers. 'I've got the agency on the phone begging me for an opening every five minutes.'

Caleb nodded obediently again. He was an agency worker himself. He'd been at the XP employment agency office in Pantyfynnon six months ago, waiting for a secretary to take a photocopy of his passport when he'd seen the advert for operatives at Cleflock Beef on the counter. The secretary seemed surprised by his interest in the job. 'It's long hours,' she'd said, raising her meticulous eyebrows. 'Freezing conditions. And physically demanding.'

'I don't mind that,' he'd said.

'Sixty per cent of the workforce are migrants, recruited directly from Portugal and Eastern Europe. You know it's a slaughterhouse, don't you? Animals go in live and come out in polystyrene trays.'

'Why are you trying to talk me out of it?' Caleb had asked her. 'The reason I came here is to try to find a job.' He'd only signed on twice and already he'd had a gutsful of it, walking from Iscoed Street to the jobcentre via the old track around Cwmyoy Mountain, avoiding the high street in Tregele where everyone knew him as the athletic one off *Made in Wales,* or Ieuan-the-underlay's boy. The advisor checking over his job search record was Donna Durdern, an old neighbour from Ninian Close. She hadn't liked him since he'd clipped the wing of her Audi TT on a scrambler his old man had bought him for his fourteenth birthday. 'Well, well, well,' she'd said reading his name off the appointment card. 'Claiming job seekers benefit now are you, Mr Jenkins? How the mighty do fall!' All the net curtain twitchers in a place like Rhosybol were all over you when you were on top, but they'd stab you in the back the nanosecond you were down and out. Ask Leon Prosser.

'I understand, Phillip,' Caleb said to the supervisor, the use of his Christian name an innocent plea for clemency. 'Of course you do, Jenkins,' Morris said. 'So if I catch you coming in less than a minute late tomorrow ...' He gestured at Caleb's place on the rail. Caleb quick-marched through the pool of bloody water, happy to get away from his supervisor's shitty smelling breath. 'That's it. Get to it, numpty,' Morris said, turning to walk back to the cutting table.

Three of Caleb's four Polish co-workers were yakking in the gangway, garbled words reminiscent of old VHS tapes being rewound. Caleb circumnavigated them, crossing through the chilled carcasses hanging by iron S-hooks from the portable rail. He opened the drawer of his stainless caddy and took out his chainmail mitt. He worked his left hand into it, the steel links tight against the lumps of his knuckles. Once it was on, the only item left in the drawer was his hacksaw. His boning knife was missing.

He spied around the primary butchering area. On top of the unattended caddy opposite him was the seven-inch blade; the white 'C' he'd Tippexed on its plastic handle and the smaller 'unt' that someone on night shift had added in felt tip. He was about to fetch it when he noticed the Poles dawdling away from their discussion. Caleb pulled back. Jan, the lanky twenty-something who worked in the place opposite sidled over to the caddy and without hesitation picked up Caleb's knife. He stepped up to his carcass, the blade thrust out in front of him. 'Hey!' Caleb called.

Jan gawked at Caleb, fierce ash-blue eyes striking against his pallid skin. '*Co?*' he said, which Caleb guessed meant, *what?* He browsed the factory in search of Lucasz, the only Polish butcher who could speak a little bit of English but Lucasz was nowhere to be found, his place on the rail empty and clean. Caleb pointed down at the knife in Jan's skinny hand. '*My* knife,' he said. He gestured at the markings on its plastic handle then pointed back to himself. '*That's* my knife, pal.' Jan stepped from one foot to the other, his overall giving off a rancid smell of old sweat. '*O czym mówisz?*'

Maciej, a tall boy in his late teens, left his place to join Caleb and Jan. '*O czym on mówi?*' he said to Jan, his Adam's apple pinballing past the purple shag tag on the side of his neck.

'Look,' Caleb said to the pair of them. He took Jan's elbow in his chainmail mitt and tapped impatiently at the handle of the knife in his palm. '*My* knife.' He gestured to himself again. 'Mine.'

'Ah,' Jan smiled, his cracked lips parting over crooked teeth. He raised his hand, offering the knife. Caleb took it immediately. 'Thank you,' he said, about to walk away.

'*Czekać*!' Jan reached his arm around Caleb's shoulder while Maciej rounded in on him from the other side, Caleb shackled to the spot. Jan took his own boning knife from inside his caddy and twisted it back and fore in the bright light, blade blunt as a hammer. '*Czy ty widzisz?*' he said.

The primary butchers were supposed to take their blades to be whetted by the knife-sharpener after lunch on Friday afternoons. Caleb never missed his slot; a chance to stand in the warmth of the sharpener's mobile van with its number plate that almost spelled *SHARPY*, away from the cold and smell of the factory floor. He loved watching the old man run the blade through his diamond grinder. On holiday in Lanzarote one year, he and Mason had met a traditional Spanish sharpy who, in daylight hours, worked from a grinder attached to the handlebars of his bike, and after dark sold ready-rolled reefers from the basket at the back. 'The sharpener will be in the car park tomorrow,' he said, guessing Jan wouldn't understand. 'To-mor-row,' he said, raising his voice as if volume could help. 'The knife man will sharpen it for you.' With that Lucasz burst through the PVC curtain, bright orange hair distinct against the ghost white wall. He headed straight for the triad of men in Jan's bay, the top knot in his hair stiffening his hairnet into a point like bishop's mitre, bushy hipster beard trimmed to perfection. 'Where've you been to?' Caleb asked him.

'For shit,' he said. He pronounced it *sheet*. 'What about you?'

'Long story.'

Lucasz said something in Polish to Jan and Maciej who responded with an indecisive glance at one another. 'His blade is blunt,' Caleb said, hoiking his head at Jan's knife.

'So?' said Lucasz.

Caleb held his boning knife up. 'He was using *this* when I got here. This is my knife. He took it from my caddy.'

'You were not here,' Lucasz said.

Caleb looked back at his empty place on the rail. 'I'm sorry but I need it back now. Make sure he gets his knife seen by the sharpy tomorrow.'

'Why are you sorry?' Lucasz said to him.

Caleb wasn't sure. He wasn't really sorry. It was just an expression.

'You said you're sorry,' Lucasz said. 'There's no need to be sorry. You are always very sorry, you English people.'

Caleb bristled. 'I'm Welsh, pal. This isn't England.'

Lucasz laughed like an exhaust pipe backfiring. 'I know,' he said. 'I am joking with you.' He slapped Caleb's upper arm. 'South Wales,' he said. He pronounced it *Vales*. 'I lived here eleven years. Before that I lived in England. But on both sides, everybody sorry.'

'I'm sorry I can't lend him this,' Caleb said, raising his knife. 'Because I need it myself now.'

Lucasz smiled, thin cherry lips pressing out of his bright ginger beard. 'I understand. I will find a knife for him.' He gently nudged Caleb out of Jan's working area. 'Nothing for *you* to worry about.'

Caleb trudged back to his own place on the rail. He stood a few moments, inspecting the heel and edge of his boning knife, Lucasz speaking to the Polish butchers in his stern Slavic language. He grabbed his first beef carcass by its arm stump and dragged it until it hung on his part of the rail, the iron hook screeching against the stainless bar. With the tip of his knife he counted up its ladder of ribs, halting when he got to the twelfth. He cut once at the thin strip of pink skin between the twelfth and thirteenth bone, this swift slash almost splitting the whole carcass into quarters. He held it by its stump again, twisting it steadily to the left so that he faced the chest cavity, his own head burrowed between the two vast racks of ribs where he made another cut to the flank, on the opposite side to his first. The lower half of the carcass was hanging by a string of spongy gristle. Caleb put his knife down on the caddy and took his hacksaw. Holding the crumpled carcass stable against his upper body, he chopped through the cow's backbone to reveal the eye of the beef; the spot where quality control would check and approve the meat's colour and marbling. It was a vivid red wine shade, two streaks of intramuscular fat knitted through it like desire lines on an OS map.

Caleb put his hacksaw into the caddy drawer. He pressed his right shoulder to the frame of the cow, a thin trickle of blood smudging the collar of his overall. Holding the chuck in his mitt, he picked up his boning knife and snipped at the only shred of sinew left holding the skeleton together. He took one short step forward as the iron S-hook jerked against the rail, the full weight of the hindquarter dropping onto his shoulder. Catching a carcass like that made Caleb feel proficient. He carried it to the cutting table only to find that his primary butcher co-worker, Bartosz, was already there. Caleb had to wait a couple of minutes for the bump-capped secondary butcher, a pretty Portuguese girl with perfect porcelain teeth, to cut Bartosz's hindquarter into shank steaks before he could turn his carcass inside up and ease it down onto the surface.

By eight o'clock Caleb had quartered seven sides of beef. The news came on the radio, the presenter talking in a gloomy tone:

Thousands have come together to celebrate the life of Jo Cox on what would have been her forty-second birthday. Batley Market Place, close to her constituency office in West Yorkshire, played host to a display of unity in solidarity with the family of the MP. The occasion was one of six held simultaneously around the world for supporters and well-wishers featuring songs, anecdotes and speeches.

Caleb's arms had been in the air since he'd arrived forty minutes ago, triceps beginning to nag. He dropped them at his sides and rested for a minute, rolling his shoulders forwards and back. 'Football now,' the presenter said, his voice brightening. 'It's been announced this morning that Wales will take on Northern Ireland in the second round at the Euro 2016 tournament while the Republic of Ireland will face France. Chris Coleman's men finished top of Group B and have been waiting to discover their second-round fate since Monday.' Northern Ireland could be tricky. Caleb scanned the factory in search of someone to share this sentiment with but everyone else was hard at work. Was Poland still in the competition? He didn't know.

A song started, a light drum tap over the same gentle piano key. The singing began in a raspy baritone. Caleb shivered as if someone was walking over his grave. In a picosecond he was back in that 2012 taxi ride home from Pantyfynnon, Savannah sashaying across the backseat, legs that went all the way up to her neck, windmilling around. 'Little red corvette,' she trilled as she sidled onto Mason's lap and smoothed her hand down the length of her velvet dress into the gap between her legs.

'Bloody hell!' the taxi driver said, watching her through the rear-view mirror, car skirting towards the grass verge. Caleb had seen her for the first time at the bar in the Lazy Hatchet a few hours earlier. He'd been checking his hair in the mirror behind

27

the spirit bottles while he waited for his change, mahogany-brown spikes sticky with styling mousse. He noticed the peroxide blonde in the queue next to him was looking at him too, bottle-green eyes homed in on him like a missile on a target. Scorching hot but obviously high maintenance, if not borderline insane. She kept staring at him until he'd got his coins and turned back into the Friday night crowd, pint of lager in hand. At midnight he'd been with his brother at the taxi rank in front of the bus station, waiting for a cab to come back from a drop-off at the student village when the blonde fell out of King Kebab on Macintosh Road. She held her hand to her forehead like a visor, inspecting Caleb and Mason from head to toe before scrambling across the road and vaulting over the crash barrier like a demented gymnast, high heels hitting the ground with a clack. 'Where're you two off?' she bawled at them, long hair falling into her face.

'Don't tell her,' Caleb shout-whispered to Mason. They had an early start on a job in Fortune Terrace in the morning. He didn't want to end up at Medusa, Rhosybol's one and only nightclub, doing shots of Sambuca until the early hours.

'Tregele,' Mason answered her to spite him. 'Why? Where're you going?'

The girl flashed a smug smile. 'Trebermawr. We can share.'

'Why not?' Caleb said. It was no skin off his nose if the taxi went through Dunvant instead of Trethomas. They'd drop her off in Trebermawr and drive up the Bryn Ivor Road home.

'You're a Sagittarius, aren't you?' she asked Mason as the cab turned onto Syracuse Road. The air freshener hanging from the mirror swung against the windscreen, giving off a pineapple smell.

'How d'you know that?' Mason said.

'Easy,' she said, turning to study his face. 'Wide forehead. Button nose. Happy mouth.' She slapped his leg. 'Long in the thigh.'

'Oh aye? What else?' Mason said.

'Optimistic but restless. Can't stand to be bossed about. Woe betide the bully who tells a Sagie what to do.'

'Bang on!' Mason said. 'Bang on.'

The taxi had stopped for a dog-walker at the zebra crossing in Hensoltown when Caleb felt something move against his leg. The girl had wedged her hand into the crevice next to his seat. 'Capricorns,' she said, busily stroking his calf, 'are a different story altogether. Ambitious, practical, goal-orientated. *They* make up their own rules.'

'He's a Capricorn,' Mason said waving at Caleb.

'I know,' she said. 'Capricorns won't make the first move because they're shy and pragmatic. But they're secretly passionate, like a volcano ready to blow.' Caleb moved his leg away from her hand. She found it again, her shoulder jammed against the edge of the seat. The taxi was passing Legacy Park in Dunvant, the old mine's winding gear and chimney lit up against the bowl of the sky when the Prince song came on the stereo.

'Oh man!' the girl shrieked at them all. 'I bloody *love* this tune.' She leaned into the armrest between the two front seats as the driver pulled up to the Happy House Chinese takeaway on Wrexham Street in Trebermawr. 'Are you coming in with me or what?' she said to Caleb, the pair of them looking at one another in the glass of the windscreen the way they had in the mirror at the bar.

'Nah,' he said after a second, turning his head away.

'Why not?' she said, incredulous. 'Don't you fancy me?' She stuck out her bottom lip, eyelashes fluttering theatrically.

'I've got work in the morning,' he said. He gestured at Mason. 'We both have.'

'Dickhead,' the taxi driver said to Caleb. He winked at the girl.

'Get out, you dull cunt,' Mason said, slapping at Caleb's shoulder. 'I'll shout you the taxi.'

Caleb got out because he didn't know what else to do. He followed the girl up a dark stairwell and into a bare, brightly lit kitchen-living-room that smelled of patchouli oil. She poured him a shot of marshmallow vodka, the drink pink and frothy like strawberry milk.

'Inni lush?' she said, watching him swallow. It was so unbearably sweet, he gagged before accidentally slamming the glass down on the chipboard counter. 'Neck me 'en?' the girl said. That classic Welsh chat-up line. She stood on her tiptoes and kissed his neck, lips soft against his thyroid cartilage; that always drove him mental. He sighed deeply, at which point the girl started clawing at the buttons of his shirt. She pushed it up towards his shoulders, her hands all over him, fingertips everywhere. He worked the velvet dress over her hips. Their clothes came off easily, like the peel of a ripe clementine slipping off in a single shred. She lowered herself onto the tiled floor, dragging him down with her, his knees hard against the cold kitchen tiles. 'Don't you have, like, a bedroom?' he'd said.

'Let's just do it.' She turned over onto her hands and knees.

Caleb looked at the vertebrae of her spine in wonderment. 'Are you sure about this?'

'Course I am, sweetheart. I've fancied you since I first saw you on that TV programme. When I saw you coming out of that bathroom with a towel wrapped around you, abs like a kickboxer. Whew. Buff as fuck.'

He woke up alone on her bed the next morning, dizzy and dehydrated, the vodka bottle toppled onto its side next to his shin. He got up and collected his clothes which were scattered around the kitchen; one Adidas sock draped over the mixer tap, the other scrunched in a ball inside his suede boot. It was when he took his shirt from the back of the armchair he saw the Ouija board balanced on the side table, the letters of the alphabet spelled out in two semi-circular rows, a 'yes' in one corner and 'no' in the other, 'goodbye' across the bottom in calligraphic script. He gasped, his puffy eyes widening in surprise. Voodoo crap like that always put the shits right up him. Ellis Gillard had told him once he'd seen druids sacrificing rabbits on an altar made from crack-willow twigs in Cwmyoy woods. Caleb had run home to Ninian Close and kept his bedroom light on all night. The girl rolled to face him, keeping her upper arm crossed over her eyes. She was wrapped in a faux-fur throw on the two-seater settee on the other side of the open-plan room. 'You're going,' she said; a statement not a question, as if she didn't mind.

Caleb let go of his breath in relief. 'Yeah. Thanks for letting me crash. I've got to go to work. I'll see you around.' If he'd wanted a girlfriend he'd have found one down the Vale or in a club in Cardiff, someone with enough sophistication not to fuck him on the first night; someone who'd make him graft, not serve it up wholesale like a bumper pack of broken biscuits.

'Where've you been, you dirty stop out?' his mother said when he got back to Tregele. 'You've got a twist pile to do today. Your father and brother have already left.' Caleb took the slice of bacon left on a plate next to the hob and folded it into his mouth. 'I hope you used a condom, anyway,' his mother said.

'Ma-am!' As he said it a text arrived from his old man: '*Late boy, shift your arse.*'

He was about to reply when a Facebook notification flashed up, a friend request from someone called Savannah Sayer. He squinted at the thumbnail photograph in the corner. It was the Ouija board girl he'd just left in Trebermawr, frosty pink lips forced into a showy duck pout. He deleted the request before dropping his phone on the dining table with the breakfast debris. 'I'm going for a shower,' he told his mother. 'Tell Daddy I'll be there in ten.'

Something crashed against the rail, the carcasses pivoting on their S-hooks. Two refrigeration workers had arrived with new stock. 'Twenty sides,' one of them said to Caleb.

'Cheers pal.' Caleb marked the number down on the board with a nub of white chalk. The refrigeration workers had disappeared behind the strip curtain by the time he looked up, the new rail parked sideways behind the existing carcasses. The Poles were bantering on, long sentences punctuated by wisps of laughter. 'Hey!' Caleb shouted to Lucasz. The man turned slowly to look at him, his white face pink with trapped hilarity. 'Did you find a knife for him?' Lucasz curled his chainmail mitt around the fleshy pinna of his ear, signalling for Caleb to repeat the question.

'Did you find a knife for Jan?'

'I lend him mine,' Lucasz said. 'It's fine. Between us we can get along. He does the boning. I do the saw.'

'Cool,' he said. Lucasz gave him a thumbs-up then turned back to Jan and Maciej, Caleb frozen out again. That's alright, he thought to himself; he hadn't come here to make friends.

A truck was reversing outside, its back-up sensor bleeping. Caleb held the arm stump of his next side of beef, hauling it along the rail before taking his boning knife to its great terrace of ribs. He made the first cut, the weight of the carcass folding in on itself. Then he made the second on the opposite side, the metallic smell of blood coming off the flesh as it slowly started to thaw. He wiped the blade of the knife against the tail of his overall then swapped it for the saw. With one well-placed blow, he broke the spine of the carcass in two. Holding the squishy meat of the neck in his mitt he took his boning knife again. With a little flourish, he sliced the band of intercostal muscle apart. The carcass dropped before he was ready for it, the forequarter landing awkwardly against his chest. He had to launch the meat up and over himself the way he used to sling Oscar over his shoulder when they were playing at judo. For a femtosecond, its weight threatened to topple him then he managed to stabilize his legs. *Thank God*, he thought to himself as he started towards the cutting table, rubber boots sloshing through the puddle of animal fluids, a thin lacquer of sweat developing under the elastic band of his hairnet.

Now there was only one side left on his portion of the rail. The boys from refrigeration hadn't been back since quarter past eight. Being able to clear the workload before the factory could deliver more work always felt like a little victory. He made a deal with himself: if he could butcher this carcass before any more appeared, he could buy himself a break time KitKat from the vending machine in the front foyer. Another *one* wouldn't hurt, not if he went running tonight and he *was* going running tonight. He'd burn a measly two hundred calories off in a heartbeat so he snatched his boning knife and urgently executed the first cuts, the blade swishing about above him like a conductor's baton.

He carried the forequarter on his shoulder to the Portuguese girl at the end of the cutting table then returned to the hindquarter left hanging on his rail. He stood up on his toes and divided the aitch bone with some pressure on the bolster of his boning knife. It must have been a young cow; older animals' pelvic bones tended to be fused like tungsten. He almost always had to use a hacksaw. He happily lifted the rear end of the carcass off the rail and walked deliberately slowly back to the cutting table, giving the Portuguese girl time to separate his forequarter into chuck and brisket portions for the other secondary butchers to work on before he put his next piece down. The girl said something in

Portuguese without looking at Caleb's face, a complex 'O' word. She sneered as she slid the S-hook out of the carcass, her top lip cockled above her flawless row of snow-white teeth. She threw the hook into a plastic box at her feet, iron clanking on iron.

'Yeah,' Caleb said.

Back in his work area, his rail was utterly bare. He wrote the time down on his board, eleven a.m., dead on. He'd add it to his timesheet at home time, so that time spent waiting for stock could not be confused with time spent working. At the end of his first week at Cleflock Beef, his wages had been docked for low productivity, not because he'd slacked but because he'd failed to account for all the carcasses that came in late from refrigeration. The corporate machine wasn't going to catch him out like that again. He heaved himself onto his caddy where he sat swinging his legs, waiting for the dead cows to arrive. The bloody water had drained away, the concrete floor, stained pink like a salt-lake. He remembered the finish at the Iron Man race, the hundreds of smiling faces lining the Esplanade blurred into a long smear of beige, the salty smell of the Irish Sea trapped in the back of his throat, glory soaring in his guts, pure and true. To be back there again. Before *Made in Wales* and Savannah Sayer. Twenty-two years old, his whole life ahead of him.

Jan shouted something to the other Poles who tiredly shook their heads.

'*Tak*,' Lucasz said to him, which Caleb knew meant 'yes'. Jan responded with a long speech full of 'ack' and 'shwe' sounds, a fast, buzzing rhythm like a bluebottle stuck behind a net curtain. Maciej howled back at him, '*Tato żart!*' Jan threw his arm around Maciej's love-bitten neck, gripping him in a headlock while he rubbed his knuckles into the youngster's cardboard-coloured hair. Caleb had noticed how tactile the Poles were in the showers. They washed each other's backs, the heels of their hands pushed into the hollows of each other's ribs like the miners in the old collieries, making sure every speck of dirt was cleaned. He felt a twinge of jealousy at this. They had something he didn't; they had each other.

Arms cold from lack of movement, Caleb pulled his mitt from his numbed hand and jammed them both between the thighs of his jeans, the glacial air trapped under the cuffs of his overall expelled. It was five minutes past eleven, only ten minutes until morning break. He was sure he had a couple of pound coins in his locker, change from the fiver he'd broken, sponsoring the cleaner to do a mud race for cancer research. Enough for a KitKat Chunky from the vending machine in the front foyer.

Bartosz said something to Lucasz.

'Oh my God,' replied Lucasz.

Bartosz spoke again then quickly clapped his hands.

Maciej burst out laughing, the force of the jollity jack-knifing his lofty body.

Jan chuckled from behind his blood-stained gloves.

Caleb's forehead began to itch. He didn't want to take his hands from the warmth between his legs but the tickle became persistent, growing more urgent by the attosecond. He was making the decision to scratch when he heard the thock of footsteps approaching. He turned, expecting to see one of the boys from refrigeration. Instead there was someone from the slaughterhouse teetering under the weight of an entire cowhide. He struggled across the length of the butchering department like a pisshead carrying a woman home from Medusa, one step forward, two steps back, pausing momentarily to redistribute the load. What the fuck? Employees weren't authorised to touch the cowhides after slaughter. They were mechanically pulled from the bodies moments after death, then transported by conveyor to be drained in the cooling room. The slaughterhouse operative kicked at the factory fire exit, the door flying open with a clatter.

He adjusted the cowhide one more time before disappearing out into the golden daylight.

'Wait!' Caleb jumped down and ran after the boy, the raw cold of the factory floor turning to the warmth of the summer day. The slaughterhouse operative was three feet across the yard, grappling with the gummy edges of the hide. 'What's going on?' Caleb asked him.

'Conveyor's broken.' It was Mykolas, a Latvian twenty-something with a mane of wispy brown hair and John Lennon-style eyeglasses. Caleb had spoken to him in the canteen a few times. His English was as good as Caleb's; better, probably. 'So what?'

'This is my last hide of the morning. I want it gone. I want to clean my bay.' He swayed under the weight of the hide, a bead of perspiration swelling below his bottom lip.

'You're not supposed to do this,' Caleb said, taking a puckered edge of the hide. He began to walk alongside Mykolas with the skin. 'You can't carry one of these on your own. You're in a factory, not Rambo.'

'I want it gone before the end of my shift.'

He must have been working the twilight. 'Have you ever heard of work-to-rule?' Caleb asked him. 'You've got to follow the rules of your contract. Follow all the safety regulations to a tee. If they see you carrying a hide around on your own they'll expect you to do it every time the belt breaks. So don't make it so easy for them.' He nodded back at the slaughterhouse. 'Do you see what I mean? That way there's work for everyone.'

Mykolas stopped walking. 'Latvia raised fifty thousand pounds for you in the UK miner's strike. '84, '85. We sent it in solidarity to pay for your food. Toys for the *bērni* at Christmas.' He stared grimly at Caleb. 'You don't believe me? Ask your grandfather! Latvia stood by you.'

'My grandfather's dead, butt.'

Mykolas let the weight of the cowhide drop to his shoulder. 'Now you're going to vote to leave EU.'

'Oh,' Caleb said. 'Is that today?' His polling card must have been in that heap of letters by the serving bowl in the hallway. He had no intention of voting. He didn't feel qualified to. His old man had a brick in his craw about freedom of movement for employers. 'These bloody factories can just up and piss off the moment they've worked out their wage bill'll be fifty percent cheaper in Estonia. And if you think *you*'ve got any rights you can think again. Strikes have to be compatible with EU law. That basically makes them illegal.' While his mother had had a gutsful of Brussels telling her how powerful her vacuum cleaner ought to be. Bureaucrats, she called them. 'It's nobody else's business how bendy our bananas are,' she'd said once, much to Mason's amusement. Sometimes the front cover of the newspaper left in the canteen after morning break splashed something like, 'Be an Outie, vote leave', and sometimes it said, 'Don't take a leap into the dark, vote remain.' Sometimes the front page said, 'Be-leave,' but the story on page four said, 'If you Brexit you'll pay for it.'

'The monthly wage is fixed at four hundred in Poland,' Mykolas said. 'In Romania, it is worse.'

'I get it. The money's good.' He didn't get it, really. How could anyone think that three hundred quid a week was good money? He supposed it must have been alright for them, they lived three families to a two-bedroom flat. They could pay their monthly rent three times over. 'It doesn't mean you've got to bust your balls. Work-to-rule. Then we all get paid fair.'

'Nothing would get done. We'd be laid off, every one of us. There are people out there, Ukrainians and Bulgarians. *They'll* work for even less.'

'Cool your tits,' Caleb said. He couldn't be arsed to argue politics. He shouldn't have been outside the factory. Mykolas peered at him, milky eyes magnified in the circular lenses of his glasses. The hide was getting too heavy to hold still. Caleb shuffled his feet. 'Let's get this moving,' he said, and together they lifted the hide until they were holding it above their heads like a shared umbrella.

'Thank you,' Mykolas said grumpily.

'No problemo, pal.' Caleb left Mykolas at the door of the cooling room and turned back toward the factory, the heat of the sun beating on the back of his neck. The light wind behind it was carrying voices on it: 'No excuse for animal abuse! No excuse for animal abuse! No excuse for animal abuse!' The protestors were at the gate again. They always came on sunny days with their banners and megaphones. They used their mobiles to film the livestock trucks as they arrived, then uploaded the footage on YouTube; shaky images of bull calves and heifers, docile eyes wide with fear. 'Bearing witness,' they called it. Caleb quietly admired their effort.

Four weeks into the job HR had offered him a promotion, a move onto the killing floor. 'What's the job exactly?' he'd asked the woman who'd come down to talk to him about it.

'Shooting a captive bolt into the animal's head,' she said. 'It's a wage increase of six point two per cent.' Obviously, he couldn't accept it. The noise that came out of there, a bleak and constant sob like a frightened toddler lost in the aisles at PriceCo, was enough to keep him awake at night. At least the cows were dead by the time they got to primary butchering. Skinned, bisected and beheaded. They weren't going to come back to life then, and wasting the flesh of an animal that had died for your sustenance would be almost as bad as killing it. He didn't want to work here at all but how else was he going to keep a roof over his family's head? All the good jobs were Cardiff way. It was either this or delivering Domino's pizzas for eight quid an hour. If he wanted to risk a stint in Hopcyn Prison he could make a small fortune dealing ketamine to the kids in Penllechau car park. The machine had the whole world by its balls.

He'd been leaving one Friday afternoon when one of the protestors, a girl with purple dreadlocks and flesh tunnels in her earlobes like an African tribesman, confronted him as he twisted through the turnstile. 'How can you do it?' she said, getting right up in his grill. How does anyone do anything? How do they get through a whole day without stabbing their tyrant of a supervisor with their boning knife? Obviously by compartmentalising – ignoring the fact that everything they did contradicted everything they believed in. He didn't want industrial-farmed cows to be turned into beef burgers but what could be more comforting than his mother's roast beef and Yorkshires on a rainy Sunday? 'Can I pass, please?' he'd asked the dreadlocked girl.

'Wanker!' she'd shouted at him before spitting a bullet of phlegm at his chest.

'Get a job, they want to,' someone said. Caleb traced this Welsh accent to a man in his early sixties sitting outside on the bench under the shower room's extractor fan. 'Alright butt?' Caleb said. 'Didn't see you there.'

He lifted his fag to his mouth and took a puff, freckles and liver spots mottling his bald head like a jigsaw missing a few final pieces. 'Where're you from 'en?' he said, flicking ash from the cigarette.

'Rhosybol.' Caleb checked the fire exit. It was still on the latch. It must be break time by now. 'And you come all the way over here every day?' the old man said, incredulous.

'It's only half hour over the Bryn. There's no work left over there.'

'Bangor Road, me,' he said, poking himself in the sternum. 'Maesygwaith, born and bred. Course my great grandfather came over from Ireland 'cause of the spud famine. Nearly dead of starvation when he got off the ship in Newport Dock. Then he slaved for thirty years in the ironworks. Proud of that, I am. Salt of the earth, the Irish and the Welsh.' Caleb sat down at the end of the bench, a ripple of tension releasing in his lower back. Mykolas emerged from the cooling room, dashing across the yard, the sun blazing through his wispy hair like an angel's halo. 'Bloody Polacks,' the old man said, watching him.

'He's Latvian,' Caleb said.

'Well, whatever you call them. They're all over the bastard shop 'ere. The surgery and nursery school packed to the rafters and another one of them deli's on Pontmorlais. All sauerkraut and pretzels and whatever the hell else.'

'What's the difference between Ireland and Poland then?' Caleb asked.

'About a thousand miles,' the old man barked, expressionless. 'Have you voted yet?'

'Nope.'

The old man tossed his fag butt into the gutter. 'Make sure you do, mush. We've got to look after our own these days. No one else will.' He clamped his hand on Caleb's shoulder and slowly straightened up. When he'd gone, Caleb sat for a few minutes enjoying the daylight and rest. Eventually he got up and headed back to the fire exit. A quartet of older Portuguese women were filing through the PVC curtain as he stepped into the frigid atmosphere of the factory, hurrying to their places on the cutting table. It was eleven thirty-two by the clock face above them. Morning break had come and gone. 'Shit!' Caleb said to himself, racing to his own bay. At least the pound coins in his locker would come for lunch. His empty rail was gone, replaced with a new set of 400 lb sides. He found his nub of chalk in the drawer and marked the time and number on the board. He was counting up the ribs of his first carcass when he sensed Morris step into the factory like a dead serial killer manifesting at one of Savannah's seances. From the corner of his eye he watched the supervisor slither over to the girl at the end of the table. He twtied down next to her, the fat of his thighs straining his chinos. He said something in Portuguese, something sleazy sounding, the girl rolling her eyes while she adjusted the peak of her bump cap. Morris was learning Polish and Portuguese on Duolingo because he wanted a job in management. Another cog in the corporate machine. Caleb slashed at the band of gristle holding the skeleton of his carcass together, the bones immediately weakening. His arse cheeks clenched when he saw Morris head from the cutting table towards him, the shit-eating grin on his face morphing into a scowl. 'Where were you before break?' he asked Caleb.

'Went for a shit.'

Morris' head jerked back as if Caleb had slapped him. 'Too much information, amigo.'

Caleb shrugged. 'You asked.'

'Are you sure that's where you were because I've had to warn you before about leaving the department in your PPE? Foreign bodies gathered on clothing is our number one cause of contamination; ash, microspores: it's a jungle out there.' He waited for a response from Caleb. 'You know we're trying to eliminate it completely, going forward,' he said when he didn't get one.

'I told you, didn't I?'

'The whole site is covered by CCTV. I could easily check.'

He was bluffing. He didn't have the time to do that. 'I had to go to the toilet,' Caleb said. 'I couldn't wait.'

41

'Okey-doke. I hope you washed your paws.' He whistled a few bars of 'Dock of the Bay' as he sauntered off. 'Wank puffin,' he said of Caleb as he crossed into secondary butchering.

'Fochrhiw,' Caleb said without moving his lips.

The meat-dicing machine started up in secondary butchering, its hidden blades rotating like a helicopter coming in to land. Caleb held the carcass in his mitt and twisted it as far as the iron hook would give. He made his second cut under the scapula and ground with his hacksaw at the spine, his mitt pressing its byzantine pattern into the white rind cladding the animal's shoulder. When it'd split, he used his boning knife to sever the last thread of sinew holding the carcass together. The spine squeaked as the carcass gave way, the hook spinning on the rail. The hindquarter fell against him like a pallet of bricks. It felt heavier than the other carcasses. Now that break time had passed, every cow would feel heavier than the last. 'There's a lot of bone dust on this one,' he told the girl with the teeth as he turned the cage of ribs onto the edge of the cutting table.

'*Pó de osso*,' the girl said to the woman next to her.

'Cheers,' Caleb said.

He was on his way back to his work area, the cold air blasting out of the cooling units stinging his earlobes, when someone at the cutting table screamed, the hundred-decibel shriek stopping him dead in his tracks. The young Polish women at the top of the table were forming a small crowd around one area of the line. One of the older Portuguese women was jumping up and down on the spot, waving her arms in the air.

'Stop!' she shouted at the women operating their bone saws further down the line. '*Acidente!* Stop the machines. *Pare!* Stop!' The drone of the electric tools died down, the words to the Justin Timberlake song on the radio loud and suddenly clear. Lucasz let go of his carcass, the meat spinning on its hook like a figure skater on ice. He ran past Caleb towards the cutting table. 'Karina!' he yelled at the gaggle of Polish girls. They parted to reveal his niece, Karina, one gloved hand balled in the other, blood dripping down her wrists onto the light blue cuffs of her cotton blouse, eyes hollow with shock.

'*Kurwa*, Karina,' he said.

Maciej chased Lucasz to the cutting table, his skeletal frame hiding Caleb's view of Lucasz's niece. Caleb skulked back to his area in primary butchering, secretly pleased with the commotion – a bit of drama broke up the long, monotonous day. Obviously, the girl had had an accident, but it was impossible to tell how bad it was. Accidents were commonplace because of the knives and slippery floor. Someone hurt themselves in butchering a couple of times a week; mostly cuts and muscle sprains. Caleb had yet to see a limb amputated by one of the grinding machines but he knew it happened. There'd been a programme about it on the telly not so long ago, how a hundred and fifty-one people had died from work injuries in the meat industry over the past decade.

Suddenly Morris hurtled through the PVC strip curtain, arms outstretched like the Angel of the North.

'Come on, show's over,' he shouted at the girls surrounding Lucasz's niece. He scrambled to the cutting table, clapping in the women's faces as if they were a pack of stray dogs eating out of a bin. They swiftly filed back to their places, faces scrunched in disgust at Morris' breath. Lucasz's niece was sitting on the mobile safety steps, a mustard T-shirt wrapped around her hand so many times it looked like a boxing glove. Maciej was crouched next to her, chainmail mitt pressed to her shoulder.

'He says she needs medical attention,' Lucasz said to Morris.

Morris looked at the purple bite on Maciej's neck. 'What's it got to do with him?'

'He is our first-aid person,' Lucasz said.

'Wowser,' Morris said. 'So he is!'

'*Nieprzyjemny,*' Maciej said.

'Alright, alright.' Morris squatted down in front of Lucasz's niece. 'Do you know where the hospital is? It's just across the estate. Five minutes in a car. We can order a taxi.'

'She's not going on her own,' Lucasz said. 'Maciej will go also.'

Morris stood up and sighed.

Behind Caleb, Bartosz said something suspicious sounding in Polish.

Jan grunted in response.

'Alright,' Morris said to Lucasz. 'One chaperone. Why not?' He turned to the Portuguese women further up the cutting table. 'What d'you think you're looking at, ladies? D'you think I pay you to gawp at these idiots? Do your work!' He signalled for Maciej and Karina to leave.

Lucasz gave Maciej an instruction in Polish that made his niece roll her eyes.

'*Tak!*' Maciej said, guiding her by her good arm towards the strip curtain.

'I pray she will be fine,' Lucasz said when they'd gone. 'I do not want to be the one to tell my sister that her daughter lost the use of her thumb.' He wiped his gloves in his overall as he headed back to primary butchering.

'She should have been using a guard on her knife,' Morris said, following him. Caleb busied himself counting the ribs of his carcass as they passed. 'Why wasn't she using her guard?' Morris asked Lucasz.

Lucasz stopped and turned to face the supervisor. 'Because it was damaged like everything else in this place. She asked for a new guard two weeks ago.' He tugged at the length of his beard, blood from his gloves smeared in the orange hair.

'I don't know anything about that!' Morris said. Lucasz stared at Morris' face.

Morris laughed in an agitated way. 'Confused dot com,' he said. Lucasz kept staring directly at Morris, cherry lips pursed. 'You're anxious,' Morris said, his voice softening. 'I get it. But try not to worry. She's in the best place. They're like miracle workers these days. It's amazing what they can do.' He nodded squarely at Lucasz. 'I'll go and check they've managed to get a taxi,' he said before he made off toward the curtain.

'What do they think *Polska* is?' Lucasz said stepping up to his place on the rail. 'Some *kurwa* country full of gypsies and savages? We have everything *they* have. Do they never hear of the NFZ? Our own national health fund!'

Caleb wondered if hospitals in Poland smelled like hospitals in Wales. Corridors steeped in disinfectant so potent it burned the lining of your lungs, and then every so often a pocket of something else; dehydrated urine or stewed Brussels sprouts. The thought of the smells made him think about Gankey Jenkins tucked up in his single occupancy unit in the respiratory ward at Ysbyty Cwm Rhosybol. That was two years ago, the last time Caleb had been to a hospital.

By the end of June, Gankey was so close to death, the charge nurse waived official visiting hours. The old man shut the shop so that they could all sit around the bed watching his skin turn pewter-grey. On a late, stale Thursday afternoon, the fast-moving clouds promising a thunderstorm, Savannah materialised in the corridor outside, fingers gripping the handles of a pushchair occupied by a toddler happily babbling away to himself. Caleb blinked a few times. 'Sav?' he said, unsure. He hadn't seen her since that morning in the flat above the Chinese takeaway in Trebermawr, a couple of years earlier. The Ouija board with its gothic letters, a sticky cup ring in the corner.

The girl came to the doorway in her jeans and polo neck, blonde hair scraped up into a chunky braid. 'Oh!' she said, her voice hoarse with surprise. 'Caleb.' She looked from him to his mother. She glanced once at Mason then half-smiled at the old man. 'I'm looking for maternity,' she said. 'My friend's just had a baby.'

'This is respiratory,' Caleb's mother said.

'My grandfather,' Caleb said, gesturing at Gankey. He lowered his voice. 'Lung cancer.'

'Oh my God.' Savvy pressed her palm to her breastbone, her manicured fingernails painted blood red. 'I'm sorry.' With that the little boy launched his rattle into the air and it landed with a crash on the floor next to Caleb's mother's Birkenstocks, three outsized pastel keys on a plastic ring. She crouched to pick them up. 'Hello sosej bach,' she said, shaking the keys in the little boy's face.

'Helen?' Savannah said to Caleb's mother. How did she know Caleb's mother's name?

'Yes, love?' Caleb's mother said, interest piqued.

Savvy cleared her throat. 'This is your grandson, Helen. Oscar.'

Mason exploded with a surprised laugh.

Caleb gawped at Savvy who shrugged aggressively at him, then down at the little boy, a chubby tyke with a bird's nest of chestnut hair and a big infectious smile.

'Here you are, sosej bach,' Caleb's mother said, handing the giant keys to the kid. She cupped her hands around his hands until she was sure he was gripping them properly. A knot of mucus untangled deep in Gankey Jenkins' chest, a splutter raising him an inch out of the bed. Caleb's parents both stood and stepped towards Gankey. The old man adjusted his pillows while his mother's hands uselessly flickered around Gankey's pyjama top.

'Anyway, my friend'll be wondering where I've got to,' Savvy said. She expertly manoeuvred the pushchair out of the unit and flew with it down the hospital corridor.

'Whiskey tango foxtrot?' Mason said to Caleb, his eyes glittering.

'Who is she, Cal?' Caleb's mother said. 'And why on earth would she tell us *that*?'

The factory hooter blew, a falsetto screech like a whistling kettle. Caleb seized his mitt by its cuff and whipped it from his hand while the bone saws at the cutting table came to a gradual halt. Lucasz barged out of primary butchering, Bartosz and Jan following him across the concrete floor. Caleb joined the bottleneck in front of the strip curtain and peeled his latex gloves from his hands while he waited to get to the wash basin, his skin soft and cold like defrosting chicken breasts. He rubbed the gooey pink soap into the webbing of his left hand with the fingertips of his right, floaters in his eyes from the factory strip lights. The bloodstains sloughed off the toes of his rubber boots as he kicked through the caustic brown chemical wash.

The locker room was full of half-dressed men speaking a variety of foreign languages. Caleb weaved through them like a ghost, shucking out of his smock as he made a beeline for his locker. He hung his hairnet and hard hat up on his hook and stepped out of his boots. He squeezed his feet into the soles of his trainers while he swept his hand across the base of the metal locker, a few dirty pound coins spilling out onto the floor. He picked them up and dropped them into the pocket of his jeans.

Without stopping to look at himself in the mirror he threw his balled-up overall into the washing bin at the door. He turned into the corridor, taking the split-level stairs to the canteen two treads at a time.

The food heaped on the hot buffet was all brown and yellow; a greasy slab of lasagne, dried-out chicken curry, wrinkled pork sausages. But at least it was fresh cooked on day shift. They closed the kitchen at one in the afternoon, the grub left to wither in its stainless-steel trays.

'Yes love?' the dinner lady said, snatching Caleb's plate out of his hand.

'What's that fish?' he asked her, hoiking his head at the battered fillets on the platter at the end. He could eat cod and plaice, but he was allergic to haddock.

'*Whas iss* fish, Kaz?' the dinner lady shouted at one of the invisible women in the kitchen behind her. 'Hake,' came the answer. 'Or pollack. I'm not sure.'

'Go on, I'll try it,' he said.

'Chips and peas?' The dinner lady pointed with her tongs at the shocking-green pulp in a Pyrex jug covered with cling film. 'Go on,' Caleb said.

He carried his plate to the till at the end of the buffet. 'That's four seventy-five please, love,' the cashier said, eyeing his food. Caleb opened his hand and gawped at the three pound coins in his palm. He showed the jowly woman on the till. 'This is all I've got. Can I give you the rest tomorrow?'

She made a clicky noise in the back of her throat like she was gargling salt water. 'You'll have to put the fish back,' she said, the loose flesh under her chin shaking. 'It's only two ninety if you get rid of the fish.' She snatched the coins from his hand then gave him a ten pence piece. 'E's bringin' 'is fish back, Kel,' the cashier thundered at the dinner lady on the hot buffet.

'Changed your mind now, 'ave you?' the dinner lady said as Caleb approached, one of the Portuguese women from the cutting table standing there waiting for a portion of lasagne. The dinner lady plucked the hake fillet from Caleb's plate with her tongs and threw it into a bin full of bread crusts and crumpled serviettes. 'There you are, kiddo,' she said.

'Thanks,' Caleb said. He carried his peas and chips to a table by the window overlooking the motorway and dipped one of his chips into the glowing green peas. One of the workers from packing, a fifty-something called Terry Eggs, was still sitting on his morning break, coffee stirrers and ripped sachets of sugar cornflaking the surface of his table two yards away. Caleb watched the delivery lorries hurtling up the motorway towards the West Midlands. 'What's a youngster like you doing in a hell hole like this?' Terry Eggs shouted after a few minutes to a pockmarked nineteen-year-old slouched on the table next to the drinks machine.

'Had to, didn't I?' the kid said, rearranging his NY Yankees cap. 'Job centre sanctioned me for missing an interview. I don't know 'ow they expected me to get all the way to Maesygwaith. Buses cost readies, like.'

'Nice office job you want, boy,' Terry Eggs said. 'Computers and what not. Clean shirt and tie.' The kid took a bite off the pasty in his paper bag.

'Aye,' he said doubtfully.

'What department have they got you in?' Terry Eggs asked him.

'Quality control,' the kid shouted back. 'Checking for hair on the calves. They're still twitching when they go past me on the belt!'

'Duw, you must have strong guts,' Terry said to him. 'Working in trim was enough for me. Boxing up all the bits left on the lines for the pie factory in Caerphilly. When a job came up in packing I got in like Flynn.' He took a slow sip of his tea. 'Do you know what I heard just now?'

'Whah's 'ah?' the kid said, chewing on his pasty.

'Polak in butchering chopped his hand off this morning. I saw the ambulance coming up the estate, blue lights going like a disco.'

'Mental,' the kid said.

Caleb looked around the canteen in search of Lucasz. Instead, he saw the brunette from payroll sitting in the alcove behind the cashier. She was gazing right back at him, her flowery red dress the only real colour in the room. They watched each other for a few moments then Caleb looked away, suddenly aware of the huge scoops of chips he was shovelling into his mouth. He stopped eating for a second then began again more slowly, methodically lifting one chip at a time.

'Anyone sitting by here?' said a bloke in his late thirties, a slight turn in his left eye. Caleb shook his head. The bloke pulled out the chair opposite and plonked himself down. 'Brexit day today, innit?' he said. 'Out, I'm voting, I'm telling you now.'

Caleb didn't really want to talk about politics but he didn't want to look like Billy No-Mates in front of the brunette either. He thought he could still feel her eyes on the back of his head but he daren't turn and acknowledge it in case she wasn't looking after all. 'Where're you from?' he asked the bloke with the squint.

'Ebbw Vale.'

Caleb laughed. 'Isn't that like a turkey voting for Christmas? All that money you've had from them.' he said, repeating a phrase he'd heard from an audience member on *Question Time*. Ebbw Vale had had more EU money than anywhere else in Wales.

'I don't give a shit about their money,' the bloke said. 'That's just refurbishment not regeneration. Nonsense and fripperies.' Caleb laughed at this old-fashioned-sounding phrase. 'A town clock that's never right,' the man continued. 'And a shiny statue of the dragon that they put on a patch of derelict land behind Bank Square. Twenty-two grand that statue cost, and on the day they unveiled it, the council closed every public kharzi in the town. What do they want us to do? Piss in the dragon's mouth?'

Caleb had to laugh at that.

The man peeled a strip of fat from his rasher of bacon and dangled it over his mouth before parting his lips and dropping it in. 'Cosmetic surgery, butt. Jobs we need, but we won't get them voting for Labour. Labour's never done shit for us.'

'Who'd you vote for?' Caleb asked him. 'Plaid Cymru?'

'*I* don't vote. It only encourages the bastards.'

Caleb sneaked back a glance at the girl in the red dress. She was playing with her lanyard, her tongue poked out in concentration, smooth suntanned skin, cheekbones like geometry. 'It couldn't get any worse,' the man said, rubbing his beer belly. 'There's families up on the hill surviving on charity from the church, like something from Victorian times.'

'Sad,' Caleb said.

'Chuck a hand grenade in, I reckon,' the man said. 'See what happens.'

Caleb had finished his chips. So much for the optimal nutrient diet. He was on 94% simple carbs. His macro count was going to be shot. 'Better get back to it,' he said, standing up. It was twelve fifty-five by the canteen clock. It was going to take him ten minutes to boot up. He carried his plate to the waste area at the back of the canteen and put it down on one of the trays racked in the trolley. As he made to walk away he saw the payroll girl coming towards him, her dirty plate in her hands. Their eyes met as they walked towards one another. Just before he got to her, Caleb thought about something his driving instructor used to say: 'Don't look directly at oncoming traffic unless you want to crash into it.' The couple brushed against one another, Caleb's shirtsleeve grazing her bare arm. 'Sorry,' they said simultaneously, Caleb's voice his customary grunt. Then they continued on in their opposite directions, Caleb too self-conscious to check if she was looking back.

The supervisor was standing in Caleb's place on the rail. A glut of adrenaline discharged from his glands like a bolt from a taser the moment he saw him lurking among the carcasses, skin the same salmon pink shade as the flayed cattle halves. 'Alright, Jenks?' he said to Caleb, tone unusually chipper.

'Yeah,' Caleb said defensively. 'Why?'

Morris slapped at the bracket of the rail. 'Change of plan.'

'What's that, then?' Caleb cracked his knuckles before he slid his hand into his chainmail glove. 'Next hundred sides need to be muscle-boned,' Morris said. 'Big order from the golden arches.'

'No probs.' Thank God he hadn't checked the CCTV. Caleb preferred muscle-boning anyway. It was trickier than quartering the carcasses, but he didn't have to chop so hard at the spine. Targets were automatically reduced by twenty per cent.

'Have you put your little tick in the box yet?' Morris asked him. Caleb scrunched his forehead in confusion, the band of his hairnet dipping down to his brows. 'Voting!' Morris barked at him. 'Have you done it yet?'

He put his hairnet back in place. 'Where would I have found the time to do that?'

'Well, we're recommending as a company that you choose to vote remain,' Morris said. 'Those numpties on the news can keep banging on about sovereignty all they like but the fact remains: no migrants, no meat industry. Simple as that.' Two Portuguese women waggled through the strip curtain. Morris looked up at the clock. 'Most people have no idea how the world works,' he said. 'Who do they think is going to pick their lettuce if the Romanians have to go home? Only one per cent of seasonal farm workers are Brits. Let that sink in.'

'I'd better check what my union is recommending first,' Caleb said.

Morris looked at Caleb like a snake had slid out of his mouth. 'Don't talk to me about unions. We don't recognise any unions.' Another cluster of secondary butchers trudged through the plastic curtain. 'Do you know where your precious Arthur Scargill lives now?' the supervisor blurted at Caleb. 'In a two-million-pound luxury apartment on the Barbican Estate,' he said without waiting for an answer. 'Not to mention his £600,000 house in Yorkshire or his holiday place in Moscow. What kind of socialist needs three properties?'

'Who's Arthur Scargill?' Caleb said. He'd heard Gankey Jenkins mention the name a couple of times but he had no idea who he really was.

'I bet your union told you to vote for Jeremy Corbyn an' all,' Morris said.

'What's wrong with Jeremy Corbyn?' Caleb's old man hated most politicians but he didn't mind Jeremy Corbyn.

'He's a scruffy bastard,' Morris said. 'Have you seen the suits he wears? Have you seen his shitty little house in North London? Nobody wants a vegetarian for a prime minister.'

'Except vegetarians,' Caleb said. Lucasz, Bartosz and Jan burst through the strip curtain and marched in single file across the concrete floor. They glared in turn at Morris as they passed Caleb's place on the rail. 'Quick as you can, going forward,'

Morris said to Caleb with a puff of his dog-shit breath. 'And you're working on an hour, remember.'

'I remember,' Caleb said. How could he forget?

'Cock womble,' Morris said sotto voce as he started walking off.

Caleb caught the carcass by its foreshank. He picked up his boning knife and diligently worked the point of the blade along the seam of connective tissue. After seven long minutes drawing his knife through the tendons enveloping the shank muscle, the first joint; a big triangle-shaped arm roast, fell out of the side into his arms with a smack. He carried it straight to the cutting table where the Portuguese girl with the teeth was busy picking the kidney knob out of a tenderloin. 'There you are, beaut,' he said, the frozen air blowing out of the cooling unit above her, stinging the ball of his nose.

He went back to the carcass on the rail, detaching the flesh from the bone with the tip of his knife, working across the brisket and chuck sections. The chuck was the best part of the cow for Big Mac meat; a jumble of muscle, fat and connective tissue, ground and packed with oil and water binders.

Caleb thought about the brunette from payroll. It had been a couple of years since a woman had looked at him like that. He'd never been afraid of a hiding off another bloke. When you grew up in Rhosybol you had to learn how to take one. But there was one kind of jab that you never saw coming. It went through your heart and straight into your bloodstream. In an attosecond it could rip out every stitch of your self-esteem. Only women could hurt you that way. What if he hooked up with her? You'd have to be all kinds of unlucky to meet your missus in a slaughterhouse. What would they say to people who asked them where they'd met? They'd have to lie and say they met on eHarmony, or in a chat room for 'truthers' like Mason and Brandy. Although nothing could be as bad as the way he'd met Savannah the second time around.

She'd been lifting the kid out of the pushchair by the time he'd found her in the hospital car park, the summer sky gone charcoal black. 'I caught pregnant, didn't I?' she'd said without moving her lips, the words an unbroken hiss. 'I know it's unusual but it happens. It happen*ed* OK.'

'You could have told me!' He'd looked properly at the toddler's brown saucer-sized eyes. A kid with brown eyes had to have at least one brown-eyed parent. Brown eyes were a dominant trait; he remembered that from biology.

'How?' Savannah had said, lowering him into the child seat in the back of her car, an old olive-green SEAT. One of the legs of his denim dungarees had rolled up to his knee. 'You blocked me on Facebook.'

'I didn't block you!' Had he? He couldn't remember. He'd stopped using Facebook when his *Made in Wales* contract came to an end. He'd never liked it anyway. Too many opinions and pictures of dogs in Yoda costumes. She'd kicked a switch at the base of the pushchair, the contraption collapsing in her hands. 'Well you never worried about it before. There's no need to start now.'

'Seriously?' Caleb had said. 'My kid.' He didn't know if it was a statement or a question. Savannah had nodded determinedly at him then got into the front of the Peugeot. She drove straight out of the car park without indicating, Caleb stood watching her, his head tilted to the side.

'I brought you up better than this,' his mother had said back at Ninian Close that night. The rain pounding on the kitchen windowpane sounded like the world coming down around their ears. She'd pointed through the downpour at the Durden's gable end. 'What are *they* going to think? I brought you up to have a bit of respect. For yourself at least.' Who cared what *they* thought? Caleb couldn't help feeling a jewel of pride swelling in his belly – he'd made something as pure as that happy little kid without even trying. The shop was closed for three weeks for mourning, an old Tregele tradition. As the idle days ticked by, the idea of the little boy began to plug the vacuum Gankey Jenkins' death had left. 'I wonder what he weighed,' Caleb's mother had said, between sips of her Bailey's Irish Cream after the wake at the Phoenix Club. She'd shook the ice in her glass as she'd turned to look at Caleb. '*You* were 9 lb 10. That was no mean feat, believe me. And she didn't have what I'd call childbearing hips, that girl I saw at the hospital. She was nothing but a dwt.'

Caleb tracked Savannah down on WhatsApp. He told her he wanted to talk. Then they'd met on a Friday lunchtime at the carvery in Trebermawr, Savannah's face plastered with glittering pink make-up as if it was a date. 'Where's the boy?' he'd asked, sitting down on a folded newspaper. He was on his break from a job at a new Trethomas block of flats, combat trousers chalky with floorboard dust. 'Creche,' she'd said.

'I thought you'd bring him.'

She'd browsed the laminated menu, the sun above the window behind her highlighting the slash marks up her forearms, scar tissue, pearl-white against the rest of her golden skin. 'What's that?' Caleb asked her. 'Did you do that to yourself?'

She hid the scars behind her hands. 'Ages ago,' she said.

'Why?'

'It's hard to explain.' She focused on something behind his shoulder.

He wanted to get off on the right foot with her so he changed the subject. 'You've got really nice eyes,' he said. It was true;

emerald green with glistening gold flecks like a cat's. He'd totally forgotten how good looking she was.

'Thanks,' she whispered. She looked at his face without quite meeting his eye. 'You've got really nice,' she made a show of studying him, 'earlobes!' Briefly, trying it out, they laughed together. 'Won any races lately?' she asked him when the waitress had come and gone.

Caleb pointed at the Just Carpets logo on his polo shirt. 'Too busy helping my old man out at the shop. I still train but not enough to compete, not yet.'

Savannah nodded. Caleb spat it out, what he'd gone there to say: 'The thing is, Sav, I want a paternity test. I want to get to know the boy, I do, but I've got to make sure he's mine.' The test had been Mason's idea; he watched a lot of Jeremy Kyle.

Savannah had glared at the notches in her steak knife. 'His name is Oscar,' she'd said.

'I know. I know what his name is. I've just got to be sure, like.'

'Fine!' she'd said. 'It's not like I've got anything to hide. You could do the test at the clinic where I work. You could do it this afternoon. The sooner the better. The results'll take a few weeks to come back. It's just a swab from your cheek, no needles or anything.'

Caleb swallowed hard. 'Great!' he'd said looking down the barrel of another life.

When the foreshank was shredded, Caleb wiped the blade of his boning knife on the tail of his smock. He took his hacksaw from his caddy, ready to trim the neck out of the chuck. It was his least favourite part of the on-the-rail boning process. The first time he'd done it he'd sawn into a lymph gland, a spatter of greasy fluid spraying into his eyes.

His Polish co-workers were singing some Polish song. They were always singing in the afternoons. They did it to pass the time. The rhythm was fast, their delivery boisterous, Jan happily tapping the quick beat with the butt of his knife against the rail. It reminded Caleb of one of the punk songs his old man used to play about immigrants wanting to sing all the time. 'Straight to Hell' by The Clash. A capella singing killed fear dead, that's what his old man reckoned, and that's why Welsh people were always at it. He stood on tiptoes to strike the blade of his saw into the blubber surrounding the cow's cervical vertebrae then carved up and down through the fat, the handle quivering when it hit bone. He turned the blade ninety degrees and sawed again, up and down, up and down, up and down.

When the paternity test had come back positive, (probability of parentage 99.99%), Caleb's mother insisted on inviting Savannah and Oscar to an August bank holiday barbecue at Ninian Close. She spent the morning stocking the lanterns with pillar candles, vacuuming the artificial grass, polishing her Buddha statue. That was for the benefit of her friend from the Tregele Chamber of Trade, Council Christine, as Mason liked to call her. Christine was married to Goronwy Lewis, the millionaire estate agent and property developer at the bottom of the high street, but had her own part-time job as a secretary at the council offices in Temple Green. She spent the rest of her time volunteering for community projects that made her look vaguely important; marshalling Pantyfynnon park runs and delivering food parcels to the old people's home in Cwmyoy. Her friendship with his mother was also a thinly-veiled interior design competition. They seemed to take it in turns to show one another around their newly-decorated spare bedrooms, mustering a warm sense of wellbeing from the grudging smile on their visitor's face. They were sitting on the rattan furniture set together, matching wide-brimmed hats shading their crepe-paper faces from the scorching sun when Savannah turned up in an old-fashioned-looking blouse, bow tied at the base of her throat.

'Well helo sosej bach!' Caleb's mother said, scooping the little boy out of Savannah's arms. She held him aloft and twisted him this way and that, Caleb watching the scene from the safety of the gas barbecue at the end of the garden. 'Do you remember me from the hospital, cariad? Do you remember your Nanna Helen?' She tapped at Oscar's nose with the tip of her finger. 'I'm your Nanna Helen! Yes I am!'

'Take it all in, bro,' Mason said from the side of his mouth. 'That's the bed you've made for yourself by there, butt. She's got you by the balls with that kiddy.' He poured a stream of his beer over the food on the grill, the liquid evaporating with a whoosh. Caleb put his own beer down on the ground and used the chef's tongs to pick up a half-cooked sausage. He held the burning meat to the back of Mason's neck, waiting a few microseconds for the pain to travel from the site of the injury to his little brother's brain. 'Fuckin' 'ell, Cal!' Mason jumped away from the tongs, one of his flip-flops going flying into the buddleia. 'I was only messing with you, mun.'

'Language!' their mother shouted at them. She gave Oscar to Christine to hold while she produced a bottle of Prosecco from under the rattan table. 'Ta-da!' She waved the bottle at Savannah who'd straightened up at the sight of it. 'Come and open it for us, Cal,' his mother called to him.

'Go on, butt,' Mason said. 'You've gorra get used to bein' under the cosh now.' Caleb trudged across the artificial lawn, hand hidden behind his back, middle finger pricked up at his dickhead brother. He took the bottle out of its bucket and pushed the heel of his thumb to the cork. He twisted it steadily one way then the other, the women pressed to their chair-backs, the same frightened look on their faces that girls in the yard at school got when a football materialised. He felt the pressure release from the neck of the bottle, the cork loosening with a pop. A thin wisp of smoke ribboned into the air.

'Ooh, well done Caleb!' Christine said, clapping her hands. Caleb shrugged. He'd learned that trick for a sequence shot for *Made in Wales*. The director had really wanted it to be with a saber but he couldn't get the hang of that.

'Why did you call him Oscar then love?' his mother asked Savannah as she lined the flutes across the table.

'Such an unusual name!' Christine said. Caleb started pouring the Prosecco.

'Actually, it's popular now,' Savvy said, snatching the only glass he'd managed to charge. 'It means champion warrior.' She raised the flute to her mouth and drank, his mother grimacing at her ruined toast.

'Well talk about spitting image,' Christine said looking from the boy in her lap to Caleb. 'They *do* look alike, don't they?' Caleb's mother said.

'Why wouldn't they?' Savvy said.

'Right then, little 'un!' Caleb's old man was wrestling towards them with the trolley from the shop, its platform loaded with a gigantic parcel wrapped in a green tarpaulin.

'Here he is,' Caleb's mother said to herself.

The old man dragged the tarpaulin away, bestowing them with the spectacle of a wooden fort-style playhouse with a raised deck, a ladder and a slide. It had working doors and windows and the Ddraig Goch flying from its turret. 'What d'you think of that, buster?' the old man said to Oscar. The boy stood up on Council Christine's lap, long arms clinging to her shoulder like a spider monkey.

'You know how clever he is with carpentry,' Caleb's mother said to Christine. To Savannah she said, 'You won't find anything like that in the shops.'

'That's insane,' Savvy said. '*Totes* insane!'

Caleb's mother took Oscar from Council Christine and handed him to Caleb, a hot tangle of arms and legs. 'Let me take a picture,' she said, grabbing her phone from the rattan table. 'All the boys with the fort.' She waved Caleb across the fake grass towards the playhouse. He stood next to the slide, arms crossed over the little boy's delicate midrib.

'You kept this quiet,' he said to the old man who was knelt on the ground in front of him, the label sticking out of his Sex Pistols T-shirt.

''Ark who's talking,' Mason said to Caleb, gesturing at Oscar as he sidled up.

'Come on then,' Caleb's mother said, lifting her mobile. 'Smiile!'

Caleb tucked his chin into the dip of Oscar's shoulder, his nose filling with the unexpected perfume of the little boy's scalp, medicated shampoo and fresh vanilla pods. Caleb's bloodstream flooded with a sudden rush of love, like coming up on a tab. 'Wow,' he said, overcome with a feeling of tranquillity so uncharted it felt like walking on the moon.

'Smashing!' his mother said, checking the picture on the screen of her phone.

Mason plucked Oscar out of Caleb's grip and lifted him by his armpits onto the raised deck of the playhouse. 'Down the slide now, butty. Show your uncle Mase how brave you are.' The boy held tight to the handrail, his top hiked up his thin-as-a-playing-card chest. 'Go on!' Mason said.

'No!' Caleb spat. The slide was too high for him.

'It's alright,' the old man said to Caleb. 'Come on, buster,' he called up to Oscar. 'You've got to try it out.' The little boy let go of the frame with a delirious giggle and threw himself forward. Caleb watched as he skidded down the wooden slide on the arse of his shorts, all the love in Caleb's guts turned to dread. That's when he realised having a kid was like trying to live with your heart on the outside of your body.

In early October, he'd taken Savvy to Cornwall for the weekend. It was mostly to give his parents quality babysitting time with Oscar. They wanted to take him to Folly Farm to see the armadillos where he and Mason had loved going as toddlers; fill him with all the ice cream and E numbers he wasn't allowed to have in Savvy's presence. 'Is this *it*?' she'd said, her voice curt with disappointment as he'd backed the Transporter onto the hard stand at the campsite in Newquay. The trees were changing colour but the weather was still warm, twenty-one degrees by the thermometer on the dash. 'Why, what were you expecting?' Caleb had asked her. 'Where did you go last year?'

'Kavos,' she'd said. 'It was amazeballs. Me 'n' Paula from the clinic. I got so hammered on mezcal and honey I headbutted a window. I had all these bits of glass sticking out of my neck like scales on a lizard. Paula met some bloke from Huddersfield with a croaky voice like Johnny Vegas.' She laughed to herself. 'It's brutal when nurses get together.'

'Really?' Caleb said, taken aback. 'Where was the boy?' He knew she didn't get on with her own parents. 'The caravan in Fontygary,' she'd said, as if it was something he should have known. 'Company for my friend Brianna's little boy.' She opened an app on her phone. 'There's a spa hotel on Fistral Beach. Couldn't we stay there? I wouldn't mind a pedicure.'

'We can't afford that.' He'd got it into his head that he was going to put a deposit down on a doer-upper he'd seen on Zoopla, a traditional two-bedroomed terrace in Iscoed Street at the bottom of Cwmyoy. She still lived in the cockroach-infested flat above the Chinese takeaway in Trebermawr. Family was family; he wanted to look after them both but he hadn't told her yet.

'I know,' she said. 'I'm joking.' She laughed flatly.

'I thought it'd be really cosy if we just stayed in the van. You could read my tarot.' She loved doing that. His reading always concluded with the three of wands. 'What does that mean?' he'd ask her and she'd point at the illustration of the journeyman on the card, 'Opportunities for new projects have yet to be realised. Try harder, basically.'

'I fancy knowing my future,' he said. 'I think exciting things are coming.'

'I haven't brought my deck,' she said, gazing at the screen of her phone. Caleb reached over his seat for the electric hook-up. 'D'you wanna cuppa?'

She picked up her warm bottle of rosé to show him. 'I've got this.'

'Fair enough.' He watched her take a swig of the wine, her neck long and slender as a swan's. 'I can do a bit of reflexology,' he said. A trainee physiotherapist at the Vale had shown him the basics between takes of a gym scene for the show. Relieve tension in the head and neck by rubbing the reflex points of the toes.

'Go on then.' She kicked off her flip-flop and dumped her foot in his lap.

As soon as he'd pushed his fingertips into the pressure point under the metatarsals she'd started warbling like a stoned Nightingale. That foot massage had turned into the best sex they'd ever had, the friction from their squabble released like a geyser. They were exhausted afterward, marooned in the front seats of the Transporter, watching the clouds rolling across the evening sky. 'Tell me why you did *this*,' Caleb said, running his thumb across the raised bumps of scar tissue on her forearm.

Savannah groaned.

'I want to understand,' he said.

'Because I was angry. I was trying to finish my degree and pay my rent. My parents wouldn't lend me any money. I felt helpless. It made me feel better, like I had some control over something.'

How could hurting herself make her feel better? That was like trying to keep yourself dry by diving into an ocean. 'You did it to spite them?' he asked her.

'Yeah, a little bit, if you want to put it like that. I'm OK now. I'm fine.' She lifted his hand from her arm and brought it to her face. She eyed him as she kissed his knuckles one by one. He understood for the first time why Sanjoy and Susmita Siddiqui from the newsagent in Tregele, whose marriage had been arranged by their grandparents, had grown so approving of each other. There was a kind of devotion, the opposite to love at first sight, in which the chemistry increased over time, a slow but inevitable burn, like a concrete continuing to harden years after it had been set.

The girl at the end of the table frowned as Caleb dropped his lump of shoulder down on her cutting board, the meat joint quivering. '*Thiẓ iẓ* tenderloin?' she said.

Caleb shook his head. 'Chuck. Outside portion.'

The girl narrowed her eyes. 'You are sure?'

'Aye. Chuck fillet, love.' He pressed his latex-gloved finger into the flesh. 'See how tough that is? Tough as old boots.' The girl nodded uncertainly. She said something in Portuguese to the woman next to her when Caleb walked away. It had just gone two o'clock when he started on the ribs. First he scraped the tip of his knife against the cartilage between the bones, gently loosening the hard tissue, then he cut along the edge of the bone's outer shell, as close as he could get without rolling his blade. He knocked at the hinge of the first rib with the butt of the knife, the blow making a hollow ringing sound, then he picked the slimy bone out of the carcass and dropped it into his bin.

As he turned to begin on the second rib, he caught sight of the Polish butchers behind him. Jan had moved out of his place on the rail and sidled towards Lucasz who was preoccupied with the contents of his caddy drawer. Jan elbowed the younger man sharply in the small of his back. '*Co?*' Lucasz said, straightening up, a startled expression on his paper-white face.

'Karina!' Jan said waving at the strip curtain.

Lucasz's niece was coming in. She walked towards secondary butchering holding her forearm above her, her hand and fingers wrapped with bandage and gauze. She shouted over the grinding machine to her co-workers on the table, pointing the bound hand at the suspended ceiling in a gun pose like Cameron Diaz in *Charlie's Angels*. Maciej tramped in behind her, jaundiced face like a slapped arse. He followed her to the table where she positioned herself in her place and snatched the piece of meat from the cutting board of the woman ahead of her. It was the beef clod Caleb had delivered a few minutes earlier. She held it in place with her injured hand, blood seeping onto her clean bandage, and said something to Maciej, tone brusque and urgent. With her good hand she lifted her knife into the air.

Lucasz slammed his caddy drawer shut and waded over to secondary butchering where he jabbed at the air and shouted something at his niece. Maciej backed away from the cutting table and quietly slunk over to his place on the rail while the young Polish girl next to Karina stomped to the box of latex gloves on the wall. She pulled a few pairs out of the slot and carried them back to the table where she dumped them in front of Karina.

Karina put her knife down and took one of the gloves, stretching the rubber until it had almost snapped; struggling to fit it over the bandage on her hand. '*Widzieć*?' she yelled at her uncle when she'd finally got it on. She stared defiantly at him.

'Do not call a wolf out of the woods!' he said to her.

The girl wagged her head from side to side, her fingertips pressed into her ears. '*Lah lahh la.*' She picked her knife up and began trimming the gristle from Caleb's shoulder chunk.

'*Cokolwiek*!' Lucasz said, throwing his arms into the air. He stormed back to primary butchering, turning the volume all the way up on the radio as he passed, sticky brown blood from his gloves smeared over the chrome knob.

The song was Caleb's old man's favourite, 'Down in the Tube Station at Midnight' by The Jam. His dad's band did a cover of it at their Sunday gigs in the Pegasus. 'They banned it off the radio,' his old man said once when they were listening to it in the car on the way back from a day trip to Dan yr Ogof. 'Tony Blackburn said punk bands should sing about trees and flowers not violence.' He snorted bitterly. 'Such a great bass line. Listen to this bit.'

'What's Wormwood Scrubs?' Mason asked, picking up on the lyrics.

'A prison. In London.'

'What's right-wing meetings?' Caleb asked. He thought it was something to do with bird shows. There was a pensioner in Alma Street who kept homing pigeons. 'Skinheads. The National Front. Idiots who think white people are better than everyone else.'

'Tyrone!' his mother said in a tone that meant *shut up*.

'Why?' Caleb asked, intrigued. 'Why do they think that?'

'Because they need someone to blame for their own flaws. Some people can only feel strong when someone else feels weak.'

As a teenager, his old man had been a member of the Anti-Nazi League. He had marched through Cardiff in opposition to the BNP and cleaned spray-paint swastikas off the toilets in Trebermawr. He was ten at the time of the miners' strike. He'd been in the cab of his father's delivery lorry when Gankey'd tried to deliver three tons of limestone from Trethomas builder's merchants to Penllechau mine. Of course the miners were stood around a fire in a steel drum at the colliery gates. 'See that?' Gankey'd said, pointing the men out. 'That's a picket line. You must *never* cross one of them,' and he'd turned his lorry around. In the schoolyard, Caleb's father played 'socialists and scabs' instead of cowboys and indians. He idolised coal miners. He always said he should have worked in a coal mine but none of those kinds of jobs existed by the time he'd left Tregele Comprehensive, so he'd had to invent his own job with an enterprise loan from the Abbey National and a fortnight business course down Temple Green. Caleb was fourteen when the old man took him on an anti-war march. He remembered it like yesterday, a wet Saturday in February, the Piccadilly Circus lights flickering against a battleship-grey sky, the hundreds of thousands of people packed like sardines in a tin, with rain-drenched banners that said, 'Don't attack Iraq!' But they did attack Iraq. That's when his old man stopped talking about politics except to say, 'To hell with the lot of 'em. They're *all* out for themselves.'

They'd been laying a Wilton in the lounge of a pub in the Gwaun Valley when news of Thatcher's death scrolled across the bottom of the silent TV screen above. 'Dad!' Caleb jumped to his feet, his tack hammer swinging in his hand. 'Dad! Look at that! She's died of a stroke.' He'd expected him to take the afternoon off to drink Guinness and whiskey chasers at the Fickle Dragon. That's what he always said he'd do. Instead he squinted over the top of his magnifying glasses at the moving headline. 'Huh,' he said. He pushed his glasses up his nose with his fingertip. 'Ding dong the witch is dead,' he said vacantly to himself before he got straight back to work. This was a few weeks after his gig at the leisure centre in Pantyfynnon where he'd called a black man in the crowd 'coloured'. Apparently the black man had been dancing like a maniac to everything they'd played, 'Alternative Ulster', 'Clampdown', even one of their own songs called 'Heartbreak Valley'. The old man was so grateful he'd shouted into the mic he used for the backing vocals on a Siouxsie and the Banshees cover: 'Will someone please buy my coloured butty at the front here a pint? And if you can't do that get down here and join him. Move your feet.'

The atmosphere in the room flipped like a switch. 'That's racist!' a woman shouted back at him before she'd drop-kicked her brandy glass at the stage and all hell had broken loose. Caleb had heard the old man talking to his mother about it in their bedroom in the early hours of the morning. 'Coloured was the polite term in my ANL days.'

'But it reminds everyone of slavery. It *sounds* racist.'

'I'm *not* racist. I'm anything but racist!'

'I know but words are powerful. You can say "people of colour" but not "coloured", not anymore.'

'What's the difference?'

'I don't know, Ieu, it's like the difference between Welshman and Taffy.'

'I don't care about 'Taffy'. They can call me a sheep shagger if they want to. It's about intent not words. I was thanking the man for supporting us. It's political correctness gone mad, Hel. That's what this is. It's censorship but they've got another think coming if they think they're going to censor me.' They didn't need to because he censored himself. He stopped singing backing on 'Peek-a-Boo'. He stopped talking about politics altogether, at least until the referendum on the EU had raised its head.

The next song on the radio was 'Our House' by Madness. The station always did that in the early afternoon; played three tracks from an old-fashioned genre back to back. '*Our house, in the middle of our street. Our house, in the middle of our...*'

Caleb thought about Iscoed Street. He remembered the day he'd got the keys, a sweltering Friday in 2014. He'd picked Savannah and Oscar up in the Transporter and driven them over the Sychpant road to Cwmyoy, the branches so dense with leaves they inclined to make a canopy above them. 'What is this?' Savvy asked as they'd stood on the pavement in front of the house. Caleb opened the door. Then he'd lifted her into his arms. He had to carry her over the threshold, that's what his old man had said. 'No! No! No!' She kicked her legs. 'Put me down. You're hurting me.'

'Alright!' He put her down on the doorstep. 'Our house,' he said, waving down the hallway. 'It's ours. I bought it for us.'

'Gass!' Oscar said running through the kitchen towards the back garden. 'Gass, Mammy! Gass.' In reality it was weeds, lamb's quarter and dandelion clocks, but he'd lived in the flat above the Chinese since the day he was born. Savannah had to drive him to Dunvant Park for him to be able to kick his football. 'Could I paint this purple?' Savannah said, running her hand across the bedroom wall. 'Purple's my favourite colour.'

'Yeah. Why not?'

'The only colour I'm allowed to paint the flat is cream. The landlord's got to approve it.'

'This is going to be yours.'

She looked at him with tears in her eyes. 'Really?' she said. 'Yeah.'

'We'll need to burn some sage. It clears the negative energy.'

'Whatever you want,' he said. He was ready to settle, get a Netflix account; the whole kit and caboodle. He knew now that at the end of it all he'd be laid on a bed in Ysbyty Cwm Rhosybol, an oxygen mask covering his face. The only people around him would be his kids and theirs. Not the producers of *Made in Wales*, not the applauding crowd at the finish line of the Iron Man, none of the V-tapers at the gym.

The house was supposed to have been a clean slate. It had turned out to be his parents' safety net. The old man would be outside now with his shovel. He'd been obsessed with the Japanese knotweed since the day he'd moved in, making it his mission to get rid. 'Don't you know how invasive this stuff is? It could loosen the foundations of the house.' As if a flame-resistant species of herbaceous perennial had anything on what Savannah had done. His mother would be at the table in the tiny kitchenette with her laptop, waiting for Council Christine's next Facebook post, her view of her post-bankruptcy world filtered through the prism of her friend's humblebrags.

Caleb looked at the clock above the cutting table. It was thirty-five minutes past two. Mason would be in the skunk-choked bedroom having Skype-sex with his American girlfriend. It was half seven in the morning in New Mexico.

The music stopped without warning. Caleb looked up to see Morris marching away from the radio, a clipboard pulled to his chest. 'There you are,' he said, clocking Lucasz's niece at the cutting table. 'Welcome back!' Karina nodded at the supervisor. He ambled over to primary butchering, checking the progress on the rails as he approached. 'How did it go?' he asked Maciej as he brushed past Caleb's back.

'Not good,' Lucasz said. 'The doctor says she will need rest for seven days.'

'Is that right?' Morris asked Maciej. Maciej shrugged.

Lucasz said something in Polish.

Morris laughed awkwardly. 'Well, what do they know?' he said. 'Technically, it's her decision. If she wants to work, I can't stop her.' Lucasz started speaking in Polish again but Morris cut him off. 'I need to get the accident book,' he said. 'It's back in my office.'

'*Dupek*,' Maciej said when Morris had slipped through the PVC curtain.

Caleb gently scratched at the fatty pulp on the inside of the plate he was processing, lifting one corner with the spine of his blade. He took it in the mesh fourchettes of his glove and pulled, stripping the whole layer from the bone. This cut would get diced for stir-fry. When it came off less easily, scored from the boning knife or ripped from lack of pressure they sent it to be mashed into corned beef. He could already see that the pin bone was wide. This meant the carcass had been a cow, not a bull or a heifer. She'd been a mother.

He'd believed Savannah when she'd said she'd had an abortion. That made perfect sense. They'd been watching the news on the telly in the house when a report had come on about pro-life campaigners harassing patients outside an abortion clinic in the middle of St Mary Street. They'd only been living there a couple of days. Oscar hadn't moved in yet; she said he was away in her friend's Fontygary caravan again. A woman whose face was blurred out talked to the camera in a hard Cardiff accent: 'I had to have it 'cause I was in an abusive relationship and I didn't want to bring a baby into such a volatile situation. I was on my ways into the clinic when one of these so-called Christians outside calls me a murderer. It was a difficult decision without him pouring salt onto the wounds.' Savvy'd started bawling, monumental sobs that shook her whole body. He'd tried to hug her but she'd pushed him away. 'I'm fine, Cal!' she'd said pulling herself together like she was zipping up a coat.

'Because he got me pregnant,' she'd said, gesticulating at Caleb when his mother had turned up a couple of days later demanding to know why the photo of Oscar she'd put up on Facebook had attracted a comment from Maisie Lloyd claiming the boy was her nephew, that his real name was Jake.

'Who's Maisie Lloyd?' Caleb said, baffled. It was late on a Saturday night. He was sitting on the broken bed settee in his boxer shorts, five Peronis down. A film was on the television. 'The girl who works in that new chip shop,' his mother said, annoyed at his interjection. 'Codswallop, I think it's called.' She was wearing blue polka-dot pyjamas, fur-lined Ugg boots on her feet, soaking hair plastered to her forehead. She'd walked from Ninian Close to Iscoed Street in the slanting rain. She must have had a glass of wine or two herself. 'Spit it out, lovely girl!' she screeched at Savannah. Savannah looked at his mother like hell had frozen over. That's when he realised something had shifted. The shit had hit the fan. 'I wanted that baby. I wanted it so much. But he didn't want to see me. He didn't want to know.'

'So?' his mother spat. She leaned back against the partition wall.

'I got rid of it,' Savannah said. 'What else was I going to do? But that was the wrong decision. That gutted me like a fish.'

'Did it now?' his mother said.

'You don't understand, Helen. Brianna's postnatal depression kicked in the day after she had him. She couldn't look after him. She couldn't look *at* him. I did it *all*. He was as good as mine.' She glanced at Caleb, her green eyes turning black. 'He was as good as ours.'

'Who was?' his mother barked.

Savannah dropped her shoulders, her arms falling into her lap like a rag doll's. 'Jakey,' she said.

Caleb sat up straight. 'Oscar isn't mine?'

His mother peeled herself from the wall. 'Oscar isn't hers.' She stamped over to Savannah, Ugg boots squelching on the floor. 'You faked that DNA test. You used the equipment at that clinic of yours to forge the results.' Savannah squeezed her eyes closed. Her body tensed as if it was trying to fold in on itself. His mother slapped Savannah's face, the force producing a crunching sound like a raw vegetable snapping, her blonde hair whipped into the air.

The factory hooter blasted for afternoon break. It took Caleb a second to work out where he was, the whirr of the bone saws on the cutting table gradually dying down. The Polish butchers filed past, their language burbling like birdsong; familiar but unfathomable. They joined the queue for the wash basin. Caleb didn't have enough money to buy himself a snack. He couldn't be bothered to shuck out of his smock only to boot up again in ten minutes' time. He hopped onto his caddy, blood dripping from the soles of his wellies as he watched the factory empty around him.

Tregele station was empty. A couple of pigeons picking at last night's kebabs. The destinations on the electronic sign board kept rolling around and around. *Trefecca, Gwynfa, Dunvant, Trebermawr, Hensoltown, Pantyffynon.* 'This is mental,' Caleb said, breaking the hulking silence. 'Just tell me why, Sav. Say *some*thing. Please.' After his mother had gone, she'd barricaded herself in Oscar's bedroom. He heard her sobbing but every time he'd tried to talk to her through the door she'd shout-whispered back to him: 'Shut up, Cal. He's trying to sleep!' He couldn't believe it. He'd had no idea. Then the splinters of realisation started to poke through: The toddler was hardly ever around. Over one Sunday dinner at Ninian Close his mother had asked

Savannah about her postnatal bleeding. 'I didn't,' she'd said. 'He popped out like a Jack-in-the-box.'

'Box!' Mason repeated, sniggering to himself. Caleb's mother looked suspicious.

'Really? Most women bleed for days.' She slapped at Mason's shoulder. 'After him I got some terrible clots.' Savvy'd blushed. 'Maybe a little bit,' she'd said then.

Caleb had fallen asleep himself at around five. He'd woken up a few hours later to Savannah trying to sneak out of the front door, a black bag full of clothes, the kid in the pushchair on the Iscoed Street pavement. 'You can't carry all that. I'll give you a lift, wherever you're going.' She hadn't touched the SEAT since it'd failed its MOT.

Now they were sitting in the cab of the VW, the dry heat from the core burning Caleb's face. 'Fine.' She pulled the little boy packed on her lap closer, eyes bugged from crying. 'It's because it was the only way I could get you. I wasn't good enough but I knew you'd want the baby. "Family is everything." That's what you said on *Made in Wales*.'

'What d'you mean you weren't good enough?'

Savannah sighed. 'You know what I mean. You've got everything. I'm nobody. A one-night stand. A hit-and-run.' The little boy slapped at the dash, his little handprint stamped in the thin layer of dust. 'I love you,' Caleb said.

'No. You love the mother of your child. You love Oscar.' As she said it the little boy plunged his dirty fingers into his mouth. 'Stop it, Jake!' Savannah said, pulling them out. 'Ych-y-fi.' The rails on the track crooned. The train was coming. 'Shit!' Savannah gathered the boy up and struggled out of the cab. She carried him over to the platform, Caleb following with the pushchair and bag. 'I wish you'd stay and talk,' he said as the yellow face of the train drew in. 'Where *are* you going anyway?'

'Take this one back to his mother.' The train doors slid open. Caleb got on and stuffed the bag and pushchair into the luggage rack. Savannah waited for him to alight before she got on herself. 'Then... I don't know, my parents I s'pose,' she said from the gangway. This was where Caleb should have stopped her. 'Wait,' he would have said, if it had been some Hollywood film. The word just wouldn't come. How could he ever trust her? If he let her get away with it he'd look like a soft touch, a right muggins. He had *some* pride. The guard hanging out of the door pressed a button on his keypad then swung back inside. A little alarm beeped three times to warn everyone the doors were about to close. Savannah carried the kid to a seat halfway along the carriage. Caleb waved at him, at the boy, the innocent, shiny dollop of life, then turned and walked back to the VW. He concentrated on yanking the cab door open while the train rattled away.

The radio was still turned to mute, the only noise a soft hum from the air-cooling system that kept the temperature in the factory at a strict 12°C. Beneath it the repetitive 'pock' sound of the captive bolt gun in the slaughterhouse. Caleb looked up at the skinned carcasses hanging from the rail, then across at the bloody body parts strewn around the cutting table. Maybe he should have gone to the canteen just to see if the girl from payroll was there. 'When are you going to start *courting* again, Cal?' the old man had asked him a few Sundays ago, as if it was the 1950s and they'd just got back from singing hymns at Siloh Chapel. 'You need a good woman to keep you busy, that's what you need.' It had made Caleb think about the tennis courts hidden behind Tregele Park; the private one maintained by Rhosybol Tennis Club with its blue

anti-slip surface and padlock, and the council-owned one next to
it where he used to go bunking, the concrete ground sprayed with
shattered glass, the nets rotted to shreds. Now he remembered
the Magistrates' Court in Pantyfynnon. That nightmare before
Christmas.

The chamber had looked more like a classroom at Tregele
Comprehensive than anything he'd seen on TV, scratched yellow
desks and hairy carpet tiles, the reek of bacteria-steeped rain.
Savannah had sat alone to the left of the district judge, her arms
crossed so tightly it looked like she was trying to crush herself.
She'd put on some weight, a soft mantle of flab under her chin.
The blonde had grown out of her hair, the colour left behind a
greasy copper-brown. The suit in front of the bench tapped his
microphone a few times. 'Ms Sayer, you're charged with one
count of making a false document under the Forgery and
Counterfeiting Act of 1981. How do you wish to plead?'

'Guilty,' Savannah had said. She didn't have much choice;
Caleb's mother had kept the letter announcing the DNA result
between the pages of a book about the Atkins Diet. When the
police came, she'd given it to them. Savannah hadn't seen that
coming in any of her tarot cards. 'Ms Sayer is painfully aware of
the distress her crime has caused,' Savannah's solicitor said. 'It's
worth noting that this behaviour was triggered by the termination
of a pregnancy that left her heartbroken. Initially her intentions
were entirely credible. She was, in effect, an unpaid babysitter
for the child she later claimed was hers since the child's birth
mother, Ms Lloyd was suffering with postpartum psychosis.
Unfortunately, the care of the child took a toll on Ms Sayer's own
mental health.'

'What's she trying to say?' Caleb's mother had hissed into his
ear. She was wearing a strange peppery scented perfume and new

peach-coloured lipstick. She hadn't worn make-up since the last Chamber of Commerce dinner at the Babylon in Temple Green. 'Babysitting isn't hard, not for a nurse.' Caleb shushed his mother.

'Your Worship,' the solicitor said, quieting the room. 'At the time of Ms Sayer's crime, she felt like she'd lost everything, as if she had nothing left to lose. She was a respected staff nurse with an exemplary record. This behaviour was out of the ordinary.'

Brianna Lloyd's mother, Jacob's maternal grandmother, stood up to read a victim impact statement. She was an old, beige woman; beige jacket, beige necklace, beige skin. 'Jacob didn't have a father figure when he was born,' she'd said, the paper shaking in her bony hands. 'My daughter split up with her boyfriend when she was twelve weeks' pregnant. My own husband, Gareth, is gone, God rest him.' She pressed the gold ring pinched on her finger. 'Jacob didn't have a father figure until he met Caleb Jenkins.' She glanced over the paper at Caleb's face, her lips stretched to a simper. 'He misses him desperately. He asks us all the time where his daddy is. He finds it impossible to accept, however many times we have to explain it to him, that Caleb wasn't really his father.' The microphone amplified the raspy sound of her paper as she folded it closed. 'It's painful for everyone.' Caleb looked down at the chewing-gum-smudged carpet tile. He contracted his obliques, holding the emotion deep in his guts. 'We can only hope that over time, his memories will fade,' the beige woman said.

A mobile had bleated in the row behind him, the default iPhone tune. After two rings, it stopped. 'Savannah Geraldine Sayer,' the judge said to Savannah. Savannah'd made to stand but he signalled to her to stay seated. 'In deciding your sentence I've considered all that's been said on your behalf and all that's contained in the prepared documents.' He stroked the notes on the table in front of him. 'It seems you have an immature attitude and little understanding of the impact your forgery has had. You will attend a thinking skills programme designed to sensitise you to the damage you've caused with your twisted fantasies and delusions. The protective order issued on the seventeenth of last month remains in motion until further notice.'

'Is that all?' Caleb's mother had spat as they'd stepped out into the rain. 'A bloody thinking skills programme?' There was a gully-sucker stationed in the car park, its suction trunk dipped in a drain next to the wall. Part of the tarmac was flooded. 'Mam, you knew she wouldn't get that much. Six months was the maximum. The girl from victim support told us that.' As they'd dashed towards the car, Caleb saw the cleaning-lorry was blocking the exit. They wouldn't be able to get out of the car park, not yet. 'And the abortion. That couldn't have been nice.'

'Why should we believe her about that? The pack of lies she's told! It's not like we've got any proof.' Caleb didn't feel like arguing. More people from the court were dribbling into the car park. The beige woman fished a Union Jack-print umbrella out of her handbag and slid it up. 'Let's go to The Earl's for a custard slice,' Caleb's mother said, taking his arm. 'I like it there.' Caleb liked it too, an Italian art deco-style café at the other end of Union Street; steel ice cream dishes and leather dining booths. It'd been a treat after his appointments at the orthodontist on Pencerrig Crescent.

'Really?' Caleb said. The last thing he'd wanted was to traipse through Pantyfynnon in the icy rain. He'd felt exposed enough as it was.

'Yep!' She'd pulled him towards the pedestrian gate. 'That's the least we deserve.' They walked under the railway bridge past the taxi rank where he'd first met Savannah three years earlier. None of this would be happening, he'd thought, if he'd had the balls to stay in the car when she'd got out. So what if Mason had taken the piss? So fucking what if the cab driver thought he was gay?

Macintosh Road was trimmed up for Christmas, a fifteen-foot fir tree propped in a crate outside the bank. There was a *Star Wars* display in the window of WH Smith; glowing blue Jedi Master light-sabers, a Lego Millennium Falcon, an interactive Chewbacca figure. He'd started crying so hard it'd felt like he was crying blood, his very life force flowing out of his tear ducts. He folded into his mother's arms, weeping like a kid. 'Come on, Cal,' his mother said, rubbing her hands around his shoulder blades like she was burping a newborn baby, her bitter fragrance jammed in his nostrils with the mucus and the snot.

He leaned behind the side of beef next him to look at the clock; three minutes to three. He swung his ankles, resisting the urge to return to his carcass. Only blacklegs worked through their breaks. He wanted to go running right now, running right out of the factory and down Derwen to the Klondyke track and field, run all of his agitation off. But he had to wait until he got back to Rhosybol. Then he'd run to Trethomas. He'd run all the way to Bridallt Park and back.

The first butcher through the PVC strips was the pretty Portuguese girl from the end of the table. She yanked her latex gloves onto her hands as she walked to her place. Caleb hopped off his caddy, the soles of his boots slapping on the film of bloody water on the floor. She jumped. '*Oh meu Deus*! You scare me!'

'Sorry,' Caleb said.

Two older women came in cackling, arranging their hairnets around their plump, frostbitten faces. Caleb took his knife from his drawer and began running its tip around the white fat enveloping the kidney lodged in the hindquarter.

'*Right-teeoh*!' Morris said, following the primary butchers into the factory, the green A5 accident book in his hand. He opened it as he approached the cutting table. 'It's all written down,' he said, twti-ing next to Lucasz's niece. He slid a pen out of his shirt pocket and handed it to her. 'All you need to do is sign.'

'*Nie nie nie!*' Lucasz raced past Caleb towards them. He snatched the open book out of Morris' hand, his niece dropping her head in embarrassment.

'Just what is it you think you're doing?' Morris said, trying to snatch it back. Lucasz held it fast, blood from his gloves smudging the thin graph-printed paper. He squinted to read what was written down on the page. 'Lucasz, this isn't any of your business,' Morris said, giving the book another tug. 'Karina is more than capable of—'

Lucasz spoke over the supervisor, reading the note aloud: 'June twenty-three, eleven-four-five approx. Wozniak sliced part of her left index performing given task. Superficial cut caused by lack of,' he paused to scrutinise a word, 'adequate!' he said finally, 'adequate attention as witnessed by Pawlak and Sawicki.' He looked up at the women named in Morris' note then back down at the writing. 'Attended to at Royal Maesygwaith A and E.' He slapped the book shut. He barked something in Polish at Morris.

'Actually—' Morris said.

Lucasz roared back in Polish, one long, winding sentence full of Vs and Zs. They stared at one another, a hostile silence descending on the factory. Then Lucasz turned to the woman to the left of his niece. He asked her a question Caleb couldn't understand. The woman moved the joint of beef on her cutting board down a place, ignoring Lucasz. He asked the woman on the right the same question. '*Tak*,' she said irritably. She curled the strand of black hair that had sprung out of her hairnet behind her ear. 'Broken for weeks,' she said. They must have been talking about the guard for Karina's knife.

'Unnecessary details!' Morris said. 'At the end of the day it is what it is.' He tried to wrestle the book back again.

Lucasz held firm. '*Czekać*,' he said, striding back to primary butchering. 'You!' he said when he got to Caleb. He showed him the writing on the paper. 'This,' he said, pointing to the sloping 'superficial' at the start of the third sentence. 'What does this mean?'

'Superficial?' Caleb said.

Lucasz nodded.

Morris glared at him from the cutting table, a look on his face like he was about to internally combust. 'It's just manager speak,' he said. 'It doesn't mean anything.'

Lucasz ignored Morris while closely eyeballing Caleb. 'I barely scraped a C in my English GCSE,' he said trying to evade the predicament he could sense coming. 'Don't ask me.' Anyway, that was true. At Just Carpets, he'd done all the calculations. It was Mason who typed the quotes and invoices up.

'You speak English!' Lucasz shouted at him.

'Not much better than you, butt,' Caleb said.

'A bit though, yes. Tell me.' He pointed at the 'superficial' again. 'What does it mean?'

Caleb couldn't lie. 'Not serious,' he said. 'Not dangerous. A little graze.'

'*Kłamca*!' Lucasz yelled at Morris. '*Whut*? Because I'm Polish, you think you can baffle me with *bullsheet*?' He threw the accident book onto Caleb's caddy. 'Karin will not sign.'

Morris hurried to primary butchering and took up a wide-legged stance next to the drain, hands balled in his pockets. 'Well if you're going to be pedantic about it,' he said. Nobody responded so he stood there another half minute wondering what to do. 'It won't make any difference,' he said. 'Not in the long run.' Lucasz turned to the rail, his body inclined toward his carcass. Morris brushed a fictitious speck of dirt off his shoulder. He looked from the accident book on Caleb's caddy to Caleb, a look on his face like he wanted to rip his head off and shit down his neck. '*Don't look at me,*' Caleb thought to himself. It wasn't his fault. 'I'll just get my Tippex then,' Morris said. He seemed to glide across the factory like a Dalek in Doctor Who, the PVC curtain strips fluttering behind him.

Maciej stomped to the radio and turned the volume up. The end of Jay-Z's '99 Problems' came blasting out of the speakers. He did a little dance in the middle of the factory, gangly arms flailing, tongue poked out of his mouth, before he kicked through the bloody water all the way back to the rail. Caleb ran the tip of his knife around the kidney again. This time he drove it deeper, gently dislodging the tendons holding the organ in place until it slopped onto the palm of his mitt; a bundle of round pods like a bloody bunch of grapes.

A new song started, a sad piano tune with a soulful mezzo soprano purring over the top: '*I wanna sing, I wanna shout, I wanna scream 'til the words dry out. So put it in all of the papers, I'm not afraid. They can read all about it, read all about it.*'

Before he could stop himself, Caleb was thinking about the *South Wales Echo* story. Parts of it were burned into his brain like the spelling of his own name: 'A besotted nurse tricked a man into thinking he had fathered a baby during a one-night stand. Savannah Sayer, 23, faked a DNA test to convince former Iron Man competitor and reality TV personality, Caleb Jenkins, that he had a son. Mr Jenkins, 27, of Tregele, Rhosybol, was taken in by a 'lie that snowballed out of control' and grew to love the boy he believed he fathered during the one-off drunken encounter.'

He'd been looking for a piece of card to fashion into a roach for the spliff he'd rolled for himself when he'd found the folded newspaper under Mason's bed. He'd flipped through the pages expecting to find a glossy leaflet promoting plumbing services, the kind of cheap advertising space Just Carpets were always trying to avoid. 'Jenkins even bought a house to support Sayer and the baby. In fact, the two-year-old belonged to one of Sayer's friends – who also had no idea what she'd been up to. The web of deceit went on for six months and was only exposed when a family friend who knew the boy's real parents saw a photograph of the child with Mr Jenkins on a social media platform.'

A bit of vomit had spouted up Caleb's throat then rolled back down again, an acid taste left in his mouth. He'd wanted to stop reading but couldn't. He'd felt like that kid in *A Clockwork Orange*, forced to watch violent films with his eyes clamped open. 'Sayer, of Trebermawr, Rhosybol, even convinced Mr Jenkins' parents that the toddler was their grandchild. Mr Jenkins' mum, Helen Jenkins, 54, said, 'I cannot think of the words to explain how awful it is that a human being could mislead someone like this. We accepted the child as our own flesh and blood. We showered him with gifts. There's a lot of healing to be done.'

Caleb had flown downstairs, the Sapele door opening with the force of his landing in the hall. 'What the hell is this?' he'd said, shaking the newspaper.

His mother had turned from *The Apprentice* to look at him, recognition in her eyes. 'Oh, I forgot to tell you, love,' she'd said.

'You spoke to the newspaper about me?' Anger was erupting out of his cannabis-induced calm like the Hulk busting out of a shirt. 'Why? How?'

'She phoned me the day after the court case, the reporter. A youngster, lovely girl. Easy to talk to. I didn't like to say no. Anyway, I was sorry I didn't give a victim statement of my own after all. I wanted to say my piece.'

'It's bad enough everyone knows we've gone bankrupt,' he'd said, purely to hurt his mother. 'Now everyone knows about this as well.' He shook the newspaper again. The energy he'd put into the triathlons would be forgotten. The baby scandal is what would be remembered. He'd gone from victor to victim in three paragraphs. They'd turned him into a Generation Y Leon Prosser. 'Tomorrow's chip paper, boy,' his old man had piped up.

'Oh my God!' Caleb had said, enraged. 'As if they still use actual newspapers!'

'Why shouldn't they?' his mother said. 'It never harmed us.' She was trying to change the subject.

'Shut up, Mam!' he'd said.

'I beg your pardon,' she'd said, faux-outraged.

'You've got to grow a thick skin, boy,' the old man had said. 'Simple as that.'

'I can't grow a thick skin, Dad. I'm stuck with the skin I've got. I'm stuck with the skin you gave me.'

'Cal,' his father'd said, shaking his head.

'I trusted you,' Caleb had bawled at his mother. 'I thought you understood.' He'd pointed her quote out, his finger tearing a hole in the newsprint. '"We showered him with gifts." Why did you have to say that? It's like it's all about money with you. It's all about your lost little empire. Keeping up appearances. Keeping up with the Council Christines.'

'It's the truth,' his mother said. 'Come on, Caleb. You know it is. We spent a lot on him. We spoilt him rotten. Six months of toys and treats, new clothes, new shoes. And truth be told I don't care who knows it. If it means that little madam can't ever go back to nursing or she gets recognised wherever she goes, it's worth it.'

His mother was willing to inflict pain on herself as long as

Savannah hurt more. 'This is all so fucked up I don't even know,' he'd said nonsensically, before storming back to the bedroom to finish making his joint.

Now that the kidney was gone, a bloody crater left in the hindquarter the shape of an egg, Caleb began work on the knuckle-piece. Muscle-boning meant separating the muscle masses by following the natural seams of connective tissue. He slipped the tip of his knife into the microscopic crevice in front of the stifle joint then began following the hairline knurls around the sirloin tip.

Morris was back with his corrector fluid. '*Righteeoh*,' he said, shaking the bottle as he scuttled towards primary butchering. He loosened the top with a twist of his fist, leaned over Caleb's caddy and ran the brush over part of his notes. He inspected Caleb's carcass while he waited for the Tippex to dry, humming a little tune under his stinking breath. '*Righteeoh*,' he said again when it was time to write over the dried fluid. 'Explain that to your mucker, genius,' he said, handing the accident book to Caleb when he was done. He'd changed 'superficial' to 'significant'. 'Go on,' he said, hoiking his head at Lucasz, who was on his way to Caleb's place on the rail. 'Tell him what that means.'

Caleb gave the book to Lucasz to look at. 'Important, like. Meaningful.'

'Well done, clever clogs,' Morris said to him. To Lucasz he said, 'Happy now?'

'*Tak*,' Lucasz said. '*Dzięki*.'

'Good!' Morris snatched the book out of his hand and took it to the cutting table to be signed by Lucasz's niece. Caleb hit the hipbone of the carcass with the butt of his hacksaw, loosening the last piece of loin. He grabbed at it with the fourchettes of his mitt and lifted it out. He carried it to the table where the Portuguese girl was using the spine of her knife to wipe bloody slivers of gristle off her board. She took the loin from him, eyes narrowed with disappointment. She'd thought she was done for the day. Caleb looked at the clock. It was quarter to four. Back at his place the carcass was finished, nothing but the blood-stained spine and pelvic girdle left. He pushed the slumped skeleton away, iron hook squealing against the rail. His tricep muscles were throbbing, a hunger pang boomeranging around his guts. He looked at the clock again. It was ten to four. A ripple of anxiety pulsed through him at the thought of the next hour. He dragged his new carcass along the rail, visually mapping his route around the arm roast while he tried to ignore the merry end-of-shift chit-chat going on all around.

The moment the hooter blew, the women were up from the table, sashaying towards the curtain. Morris swaggered past the queue for the washbasin, heading to primary butchering. 'Hang on, boys,' he said, blocking the Polish men's path across the factory. He asked them a question in Polish, tone urgent.

'Overtime?' Lucasz said, sceptically. 'Today? I do not think so.'

'*Naprawdę?*' Morris said. 'It's time and a half. Thirteen-fifty an hour.'

Lucasz raised his eyebrows. He said something in Polish to the others.

The three men shook their heads in unison. '*Zajęty,*' Jan said.

'*Beezy,*' Lucasz said, translating for Morris. 'All of us.' As he said it, he caught Caleb's eye through a gap in the carcasses and winked.

Morris clenched his fists. 'Bugger it,' he said, punching the air at his sides. He stepped reluctantly to the right, letting the Polish men through. 'I'll remember this, boys,' he said as they passed. 'I'll remember this. Believe you me.'

'Sorry,' Lucasz said coolly as he led the others to the queue for the washbasin like a hipster pied piper.

Morris cold-eyed Caleb before gesturing at the vacant cutting table. 'Leave the merch at the end as usual,' he said. 'The twilight shift can deal with it when they come in at six.' Caleb nodded. Morris stormed back to the chaos at the PVC curtain.

'Sunshine and showers for Scotland and Northern Ireland, drier and brighter elsewhere,' said the news reporter, monotone voice reverberating around the hollowed-out factory. Tom Petty's 'I Won't Back Down' came on, Caleb instantly recognising the slide guitar intro. It was one of a handful of songs on the karaoke machine down the Unicorn. He heard it every Thursday and Friday night when he was trying to fall asleep. It was like the sound of his own thoughts, the sound of the inside of his head. He pictured himself crossing the Mumbles triathlon finish line, while he sang along, windburnt and saddle-sore but euphoric in triumph, a big grin on his face. It'd be sweeter this time around, knowing he'd got up again after being KO'd, that he'd gone back to competing like Spyro with a Fairy Kiss powerup; his enemies trapped in blocks of ice while he sped on ahead. Like Joe Calzaghe getting into his groove to win the light heavyweight championship after Bernard Hopkins hit him down in the first round. Joe Calzaghe, Super Joe. Not Leon Prosser, down and out. He could do anything he wanted if he put his mind to it. He could get the carpet shop back in the end. Just keep up keeping up with the mortgage payments so he had the house to secure a loan against. *Guess who's back? Back again. Caleb's back. Tell a friend.* If he could just catch a break he knew he'd hit the ground running, an accumulator on the Euro semi-finals or a bank error in his favour. Even Monopoly had a community chest.

He held the chuck of the carcass steady in his mitt while he struck at the ribcage with the butt of his saw. The portion of flesh he expected to drop out stayed in its cavity in the forequarter. He lifted it by its corner with the tip of his boning knife then continued with his hand, the bloody tissues parting with a wet slurp, the slimy heart-shaped cut falling into his forearms. He carried it over to the deserted cutting table. As he turned to head back to primary butchering, he saw a small crowd of people standing around his caddy, men in raspberry hi-vis. His first thought was that the protestors had managed to get into the factory. But these men were as headless as the ISIS hostages in Mason's video clips, swaying lingeringly from side to side, the way the zombies on *The Walking Dead* shifted. 'The fuck?' he said. He blinked. In a millisecond the red of the men's bibs morphed into the flanks of beef sides hanging on the rail. 'Stupid,' he said, chiding himself as he treaded cautiously across the slippery floor. He must be tireder than he thought.

At the stroke of five, he threw his sharps and mitt into the caddy and headed to the exit, a half-butchered side left suspended from his place on the rail, his timesheet left unmarked. He turned the radio off as he passed it, the news report ending abruptly. He peeled his latex gloves from his hands and threw them into the bin. The splashes from the chemical wash echoed against the silence as he waded through the piss-coloured trough. He shucked out of his smock. He tore the hairnet from his head as he stepped into the changing room, the cold from the factory settled in the honeycomb of his bones.

He opened his locker before he turned to the row of three sinks on the opposite wall. He ran the water, in the one that worked, until it began to steam, then splashed some of it onto his face, the tufts of brown sweat-matted hair at his temples softening. He grabbed the worn towel from his rucksack and rubbed it into his skin, the clothesline-dried cotton rough as sandpaper against a patch of acne developing under his stubble. He was stuffing the towel back into his bag when he saw the WhatsApp alert from Mason on his phone. He sat down on the bench to take his boots off while he read it: 'REAL EYES REALISE REAL LIES.' He snorted in response. He was about to compose a retort when he caught something red in the corner of his eye. Morris was standing in the doorway watching him, the skin of his arse on his face. Caleb recoiled in fright. 'You're still here,' he said. 'I thought you'd gone.'

'No.' Morris stepped into the changing room, his hands on his hips. He didn't say anything so Caleb continued removing his boots. He put his trainers on.

'What?' Caleb said, realising Morris was still staring at him.

'"What?" he says,' Morris said to nobody. Caleb sprayed his armpits with deodorant. 'I checked the CCTV,' Morris said after a moment. Caleb's heart sank. 'You left the factory via a fire exit at five minutes past eleven today. That's a clear breach of all the covenants in your contract—'

'I had to help Mykolas carry a cowhide to the cooling room,' Caleb interrupted. 'The conveyor's broke.'

Morris sniggered. 'Are you having a giraffe? That's not your frigging job.'

'I didn't have any work. Refrigeration were late bringing my new rail. He couldn't carry a whole skin on his own. You know how much them things weigh.'

'No I don't!' Morris spat at Caleb. 'I don't know how much they weigh because I don't make a habit of muscling in on other people's responsibilities. He shouldn't have been carrying a skin through the factory. It's against the rules, the bloody pillock. He should know as well as you do: leaving your department in your PPE is a major source of contamination.'

Caleb took a breath. 'I was only trying to help.'

'*I was only trying to help*,' Morris said, trying to mimic Caleb's baritone voice. He sounded more like Trevor off the Trade Centre Wales radio adverts.

'There's no need for that,' Caleb said, insulted.

'Don't tell me what there's a need for,' Morris bellowed. '*I'm* the supervisor.' He jabbed his gloved finger into Caleb's sternum, stamping a smudge of rusty blood onto his Just Carpets polo shirt. Before he knew what he was doing, Caleb had Morris' scrawny wrist in the air. He lowered it with a heave back to Morris' side.

Morris looked up at the camera lens fixed in the cornice. 'I'll have you for this, cockwomble.'

'Look,' Caleb said. This was getting ridiculous. *Cockwomble?* 'I'm sorry. I didn't mean to—'

'Come and see me in my office first thing in the morning,' Morris said, talking over him. 'We're due a little chinwag.'

'No!' Caleb said, thinking about the house in Iscoed Street. The house was the only thing his family had left. It was a shit house but it was their house. *Their house, in the middle of their street.*

'No?' said Morris.

Caleb swallowed hard. He had some pride. 'If you're going to sack me, do it now.'

'I didn't say I was going to sack you, did I?' Morris said. *Thank God*, Caleb thought. 'I don't have the authority to do that without Trudy Watkins from HR present. She'll be back tomorrow so come up to my office first thing and we'll see.' He stormed out of the changing room, the overhead door hinge banging like a gunshot.

'Bollocks!' Caleb said. He punched his locker door closed, his knuckles crunching against the steel. The force of the blow blasted it open again. Caleb hit it again with a right hook. *Bam.* This time the latch caught. He gave the locked door an uppercut, the metal shaking on its hinges.

He was out of the factory and running for the gate, his rucksack bouncing on his shoulder when he heard another ding-ding alert from WhatsApp. He fished through his bag for his phone as he twisted through the metal grille and out to freedom. Shielding his eyes from the early evening sun, he read another message from Mason as he crossed the empty staff car park. 'LIES HAVE LITTLE LEGS.' Another message appeared below it; a photograph of the sea hitting the horizon, blue on blue. Underneath it Mason had written 'NO CURVE!!!!' Caleb's pace increased as he reached his car parked on the kerb behind the entrance to the rubbish tip. He let his rucksack slide down his shoulder as he walked around to the driver's side. A yellow DVLA clamp was fastened with a closed-shackle padlock to the front wheel. 'The fuck?' he said, eyeing the mild steel chains on either side. He seized the plastic envelope from under the wiper and ripped it open with his teeth. 'Do not attempt to move this untaxed vehicle. Ring 0845 515 9042 for release instructions.' How could he have forgotten to pay his tax? He hadn't had a reminder. He usually got a letter in the post. He remembered the pile of unopened letters on the cupboard in the hallway. His phone was still in his hand. He poked at the numbers with a stiff index finger, then waited for an automated voice to list his options while he kicked stone chippings into a pothole in the road, the tendons in his stomach twisting like ribbon cable. 'How do I get this clamp off my car?' he said as soon as he was through to a real person. 'I'm stuck on Derwen Uchaf. I need to get home.'

'Sir, your vehicle's been clamped because it isn't currently taxed. You'll need to pay the tax.' It was a woman's voice, sweet and molten as caramel.

'I would have paid my tax if I'd got a reminder. You usually send a reminder.'

'You should have had a reminder,' she said. 'But it's your responsibility to make sure your tax is paid.'

Caleb kicked the clamp. 'How much is it?'

'One-four-three for six months. Two-sixty for the year.'

'If I pay six months you'll take the clamp off?'

'Plus the hundred pound release fee.'

'Two hundred and forty-three?' Did he have that much credit left on his card?

'Yes, sir.'

'How long will it take to get the clamp off? I need to get back to Tregele.'

'That's the good news,' the girl said, happy as a middle-class kid on Christmas morning. 'The enforcement officer is still working in the area. He shouldn't be longer than forty minutes. Can you give me the long number on the front of your card, please?' Caleb gave her the numbers. 'That's gone through for you now,' she said after a lengthy pause.

'Brilliant,' Caleb said. That'd be his card maxed for the foreseeable. He cranked the car door open and threw his rucksack into the back. He slumped into the seat, his head pressed to the steering wheel. He squeezed his eyes closed until he saw little white stars exploding in the back of his head. After a few minutes, a flatbed lorry came thundering out of the rubbish tip, the car's chassis trembling. Caleb rubbed the heels of his hands into his eye sockets. Instinct told him to move the car ten metres down the kerb, out of sight of the few staff members leaving the slaughterhouse car park, but he was stuck there like a spare prick at a wedding, the yellow clamp shining brighter than the sun.

The wind was picking up, an empty crisp packet flying across the otherwise motionless business park. His phone dinged with a new WhatsApp message from Mason. 'GRAVITY DOESN'T EXIST. THE ONLY TRUE FORCE IN NATURE IS ELECTROMAGNETISM. AUSTRALIA IS A HOAX.'

'Grow up, Mase,' Caleb typed back to him. 'Fat Gary's been to Australia. He's got a photo of himself on his mantelpiece, standing in front of Ayer's Rock.'

'That's a secret mountain range in South America, not Australia. He thinks he's been, but even all the airline pilots are in on the HOAX!!'

Caleb sent him the see-no-evil monkey emoji.

Mason sent the facepalm emoji back. 'EDUCATE URSELF, BRO!'

A crunching sound across the car park made Caleb look up. Phillip Morris was getting into his Nexus, his hard hat replaced with a black baseball cap advertising the 2010 Ryder Cup. He started his engine and manoeuvred out of his space, ugly mug pushed close to the windscreen. Thank God he didn't look in Caleb's direction as he turned out of the car park. 'Should've gone to Spec Savers,' Caleb said, watching his back bumper disappear down the hill.

A gust of wind blew against the car's window, the autoglass contracting with a pop. Caleb put his key in the ignition, the Young Fathers CD starting anew with its lunatic synthesizer. It was 17:49 by the clock on the dash. The chocolate from a half-eaten KitKat had melted into the cupholder. How was he meant to go out running now? His whole body was irritable with nervous tension, his muscles fatigued from eight hours at the rail. It was like the whole world was conspiring to stop him improving his race time. He pressed the eject button on the stereo and threw the Young Fathers CD into the glovebox. In its place, he put on an old favourite; *Encore* by Eminem. He forwarded to the fifth track, the song starting up with its military drum beat. It was now 17:53 by the clock on the dash. Caleb was dying for a slash, his bladder inflated like an airbag against his prostate. He should have gone before he left the factory but he didn't know he was going to be stuck in the car park for an hour and counting. *Fuck it*, he thought. He got out and slowly walked towards the back of the car. He undid the zip of his jeans and quickly yanked his dick out of his boxers, aiming the stream towards a clump of grass growing through the crack between the kerb stones. It was at that moment a white box van materialised, the DVLA logo sign written on its side. Caleb forced the pee to stop. He hitched up his zipper and tried to look casual as he returned to the front of the car, hands crammed in his pockets. A bloke in his mid-forties with salt-and-pepper hair got out of the van, a bunch of keys in his hand. Without looking at Caleb, he walked to the car and crouched down next to the clamp.

Caleb's piss was running down the kerb in a fast-moving rivulet, the colour of Lucozade. He stamped the sole of his trainer into the liquid to slow it while the enforcement officer messed around with the padlock.

'There we are,' he said after a minute, the chains dragging on the tarmac as he pulled the clamp away from the wheel. 'Do I need to sign anything?' Caleb asked him.

'Nah, you're alright.' He looked curiously at Caleb, a hint of recognition in his face. 'Do I know you from somewhere? I know you, you're famous. Off one of those reality efforts.'

Caleb shook his head. 'Nah, not me, mate.' He got back into the car and fastened his seatbelt. 'Come on butt,' he said, trying to chivvy himself as he shifted the gear stick into first. It was 18:10 by the clock on the dash as he drove unsmiling past the Fochrhiw signpost.

Rush hour was over. The single carriageway was clear all the way to Hebron, the fields either side of the road dotted with dappled grey ponies, the peaks of the Beacons falling away in the rear-view mirror. Caleb was flying on autopilot until he got to the Bryn bypass. There a Fiat Doblò, the colour of cat shit, couldn't have been doing more than 40 on a 60 mph stretch. Caleb slid up to the back of it, front bumper to tail, willing the old man driving to put his foot down. The road was rounded all the way; Caleb couldn't see far enough to overtake. The Doblò seemed to decelerate in response. Caleb clenched his jaw and tailgated it to the roundabout where he'd seen the dead body, the Doblò taking the second exit into Bryn village. Caleb veered left, muscles relaxing as he moved into third then quickly into fourth, speeding up the mountain approach. The little car was so close to the ground he could feel the grit against the tyres when he cornered on the bends.

The reservoir below him was a perfect mirror for the sun and clouds. Flying down a pulley above that view would be epic, Caleb thought. But it would never happen. The old man had told him about a theme park that had opened in Trefecca in the 1980s, a Wild West-style place based on Dollywood in the Smoky Mountains. It had a saloon bar and a cowboy gun-slinging show, Country and Western bands playing live every weekend. It didn't last three months. The locals couldn't afford a luxury like that back then, and Cardiffians wouldn't come to the Valleys for anything. A sheep with a purple marker on its neck was loitering at the edge of the road. Caleb slowed until he'd passed her then sped up again, the blinged-up Christmas tree in the picnic area streaming by in a blur of green and gold.

The handful of shops on the main road in Trehumphrey were

closed. A small queue of little kids in crisp white karate outfits were waiting outside the Welfare Hall. He could see something going on in the middle of the high street as soon as he crossed into Tregele, three teenagers with their hoods up facing down a couple of hobby bobbies outside Siddiqui's newsagent. Caleb branched into the right-hand lane of traffic waiting at the lights on Pegasus Square. Through his rear-view mirror he saw Susmita bust out of the shop, a fuchsia-pink sari over ripped blue jeans. She was squaring up to one of the kids, hands balled to fisticuffs like an eighteenth-century pugilist. She'd always been a girl and a half – she'd kicked his arse a few times on the football pitch behind Trefecca PriceCo. It was hard to tell from here if the quarrel was about racism or shoplifting. She had no tolerance for either. The traffic light turned green and Caleb followed the car in front of him over the hump of the bridge, stomach flipping like a fortune-telling fish.

He pulled up in front of the house in Iscoed Street and plucked his key from the ignition. Without properly acknowledging the old man who was watching something on the telly, the living room curtains drawn, Caleb dropped his rucksack on the armchair and went into the kitchenette where his mother was hunched over the sink, the Cornish flag tea towel he'd got from Newquay in her hand. 'Where've you been, Cal?' she said without turning to look at him. 'It's the twenty-third! You know: Gankey died two years ago today. I wanted you to take me to the cemetery.' Caleb remembered the flowers he'd seen on the worktop.

'Shit! Sorry, Mam! I had to work on a couple of hours. Supervisor wouldn't take no for an answer.' He didn't want to tell her about the clamp. She'd only bollock him for not paying his tax.

'It's alright. Your father took me in the end.' If it was the anniversary of his grandfather dying then it must have been the anniversary of Savannah Sayer coming briefly back into his life as well. Is that why he'd thought about her so much at work today?

'Look,' his mother said. She sidled to the table and opened the lid of her laptop. There was a photo on the screen of his grandparents' headstone. *In Loving Memory of Martha Lynn Jenkins, died 18th February 2010. Her husband Robin, died 23rd June 2014.* The flowers spewing out of the granite urns at either side. 'Mind, we should never have chosen this dark grey. It's like a magnet for seagull poo.' She threw the tea towel onto the draining board and nodded at a saucepan on the worktop. Handful of chips by there. Ham in the fridge. You'll have to open a new tin of beans.'

Caleb squeezed around her and flicked the chip fryer on at the socket. As he turned to open the fridge, he saw the photograph again on the laptop, the blue Facebook pennant in the background. 'Have you got that up on the internet?' he asked her as he reached for the block of jellied meat.

'Yeah. Why? What's wrong with that? Christine puts pictures of her mother's grave up all the time. She's got everything up there, teddy bears, windchimes, even a solar light.'

'What does she need a light for? Does she go up there in the night?' He dropped the chipped spuds into the fryer, the hot fat sizzling.

'It's just decoration, Cal. People grieve in different ways.'

He cracked the ring pull on the beans. 'It's not for her mother, is it? It's for her followers on that school reunion from hell.' He waved at his mother's laptop. 'It's for the Facebook likes.' He dumped the beans onto a plate and bunged them in the microwave. 'All those flowers must have cost a bomb,' he said eyeing the screen. 'You never bought flowers for Gankey when he was alive.' When his food was ready he put the plate down on the table, anaemic chips sprinkled with the burnt bread crumbs left in the fryer, cured ham slices floating in bright orange sauce. 'A meal fit for a king,' he said lifting his knife and fork.

'What do you expect on a Thursday teatime?' his mother said. 'T-bone steak? Black Forest gateau? Maybe a prawn cocktail to start, is it?' Caleb laughed. Steak and chips was as fancy as it got for her. She'd never heard of falafel or lychees or baked avocado or cauliflower rice. She closed the lid of her laptop. 'Are you going to vote? You know better than anyone the damage all these immigrants are doing.'

'What immigrants? This is Rhosybol, Mam. Not even immigrants want to come here.'

'Your factory. You told me yourself, you're the only English speaker there.'

'Don't be so right wing, Mam,' Caleb said.

'Right wing myn uffern i. I'm not prejudiced, Caleb. You know I'm not like that. But we need better border controls now. There's no jobs left for anyone else. Your brother can't find a job for love nor money. Your father isn't working.'

'Mason's a lazy bastard!' Caleb laughed. His mother didn't. 'And Dad is… you know.'

'Ill,' his mother said.

'Besotted with that Japanese knotweed. It's not like he can't do any physical work.'

'You know what the doctor said. The duration of a nervous breakdown varies by individual.'

'Anyway immigrants can't just turn up and demand a job. You realise that, don't you? Someone's got to give it to them.'

'Well, you should be in full-time work, the pair of you. A job is the least you should have, young fit men like you two.'

She looked into his eyes, her mouth stretched into a sad smile, the lines at either side prominent in the light from the window. He saw the outline of his body reflected in her pupils, his fork in the air in front of him. He felt suddenly dizzy, like someone had shuffled the cards of his life and they'd fallen down in a different order. If he got the sack he'd lose the house. He'd be homeless. They all would. 'Yeah,' he said absently. He got up and carried his plate to the draining board, cutlery squawking against the china.

On the screen in the living room, a man in a Dai cap and gabardine jacket cocked a Lee Enfield rifle. Caleb sat down on the settee next to the old man. 'Alright?' his dad said without looking away from the screen. The scene switched to a flashback: the Welsh actor who'd played Brian Clough in *The Damned United* speaking to the Dai cap, voice low and intense: 'There's something else you might have to do, something you will find difficult, because collaboration cannot be tolerated.' The picture switched back to the present time, the Dai cap brooding over the barrel of the gun before pulling the trigger. *Crack*.

'What's this 'en?' Caleb asked the old man.

'Film on last night,' he said. 'It was on too late to stay up.' Mason came in and threw himself onto the armchair, eyelids red and swollen. 'It imagines what Britain would've been like if Germany had invaded,' the old man said. 'The Wehrmacht knew about the plans for D-Day. Dad's Army are getting a hammering and Nelson's Column's going back to Berlin for a victory trophy.'

'I thought Germany did invade us,' Mason said. 'I thought Germany won the war.' The old man glared at him. 'I'm serious!' Mason said. 'Isn't that what this EU vote is all about?'

Caleb sniggered. 'Do you honestly think we'd be talking in English if Germany had won the war?'

'I could have done German in school,' Mason said. 'Mammy wanted us to do Welsh. I mean, everyone's driving Beamers and

Audis. All our shops are Lidls and Aldis. When we used to go to Spain, everyone moaned about the Germans getting to the pool before them. We've got a chip on our shoulders about Germany, right? I thought it was 'cause they'd won.'

'Jesus fuck,' their dad said under his breath. 'They may as well have, the state of this country. The state of you pair. There's him,' he waved dismissively at Caleb. 'Reality TV star father to a baby that doesn't exist. And you,' he waved at Mason, 'in a conference video relationship with a semiautomatic-loving Donald Trump supporter.'

'Brandy doesn't support that arsehole,' Mason said. 'She's a member of an online community called Eyes Wide Open. It's non-political.'

The old man shook his head. 'I blame Blair and Bush. They've torn the world into two extremes with their fake wars. We've got Mosleyites or snowflakes, and nothing sensible in between. The working classes used to have real clout in Britain. Now it's these champagne socialists, these neoliberals with their degrees in media studies and hedge-fund management who think they can tell everyone else how they ought to live.'

'The NWO,' Mason said. 'The New World Order, the Bilderbergs.'

'Who the bloody hell are *they* when they're at home?' the old man said.

'The free-market capitalists who run the world. Your Rockerfellers, your Clintons. NASA, HSBC. They sit in a room together once a year and plan how they're going to organise the world. They've got control of every computer system on the globe.'

'You bloody bonehead!' the old man spat at him. 'Do you tell the desk jockeys interviewing you for jobs all this stuff about NASA, Mase? 'Cause that would explain a lot.'

'Course I don't,' Mason said.

'You said "globe",' Caleb said.

'What?'

'You said the capitalists've got control of every computer system on the *globe*. I thought the earth was flat.'

Mason rolled his eyes. 'Piss off, Cal.'

'I am,' he said. He reached around his brother for his rucksack. 'I'm going out for a run.'

The springs of the bed settee chirped as Caleb sat down. He pulled on the end of his shoelace, releasing the dirty bow holding his right trainer together. Then he fell back on the cushions and gawked at a dimple in the plaster on the ceiling, his spinal cord slackening. He could have slept then and there. He needed a good night's rest; he needed to be refreshed and alert, ready to face Morris in the morning.

Then he remembered something from back in the day, a night out with the two Joshes. They'd only just turned sixteen, the three of them stewed on a bottle of Apple Sourz, psyched they'd managed to slip past the bouncer on the door at Medusa. They couldn't believe what they were seeing; girls in tops that barely covered their tits, the DJ blasting that Pussycat Dolls song with the Busta Rhymes rap on it. They'd spotted Leon Prosser in a recess in the back corner, surrounded by a group of women, orange as plastic Halloween pumpkins. He'd been clenching his jaw and grinding his teeth; it looked as if he was chewing the flesh on the inside of his cheeks. As they'd got closer they could see the sheen of sweat on his skin. He'd looked smaller in real life than he did on the telly, black eyes glassy as marbles. 'Alright butt?' Prosser'd said, calling out in Caleb's direction while the

Joshes argued over which one of them had a better chance of getting served at the bar. Obviously, Prosser couldn't have been talking to Caleb, so Caleb ignored the question. 'Alright butt?' Prosser yelled again, gesturing for Caleb to approach him. He was on his own by now, the orange women trickled away. 'What's your name 'en, butt?' Prosser had said as Caleb sidled up to him. Before Caleb could answer Prosser said, 'Look, I don't want to sound like an arrogant cunt or anything but I'm probably the most successful guy in this club. I'm probably the most successful guy you'll ever meet. You've never met a world number one before, have you? I'm a snooker player, see. I'm a snooker player, I am.'

'I know,' Caleb told him.

'No, I mean I'm a snooker player,' he'd shouted into Caleb's face. 'Professional. Main Tour. A *real* snooker player. I'm a—' Strings of vomit, off-white and gluey, like warm Ready Brek, gushed out of his mouth and nose onto Caleb's face and throat; a stink on it like fortnight-old bin juice.

He got up off the bed settee and kicked his trainers off. He swapped his work jeans and polo shirt for shorts and a singlet. He put his trainers back on and set the app on his phone to track. He wedged the phone into his shorts' pocket as he started down the stairs. The street was quiet, the hanging baskets on the house across the road swaying in the wind, the heron nest behind the garages empty. An ice cream van was on its way down the village, playing a reedy 'Waltzing Matilda'. Caleb wondered if it was really ice cream the van was selling. It had to be eight o'clock by now; most kids were in bed. Oscar was always in bed by half seven in the evening. He broke into a slow jog, lurching towards the little alleyway that cut through the back gardens, then the steps down to the main road.

A few boys in jogging bottoms were sitting on the middle

tread, torsos gathered around the screen of a mobile phone. Caleb sprang down the steps through their cloud of blue fag smoke. 'Run, Forrest, run,' one of them shouted after him in a bad American accent as he rounded the bend onto the one-sided street below. The traffic lights on Pegasus Square had changed, a flurry of cars heading to Cwmyoy. Caleb had to stop and wait for them to pass, the splinter of momentum he'd accrued on the steps already ruined. He strode up the slope to the junction where the Pontio Mountain Road met the Sychpant, building to a jog again as he skirted around the blackberry bushes. The berries were hard, green capsules encased in white petals. He came upon the old Gorsedd Circle, the jagged stone slabs stuck like giant tombstones out of the hill overlooking Tregele. He thought about Oliver West, his friend from junior school. They used to play here in the summer holidays. 'Wait,' Oliver would hiss, his arms dramatically outstretched to hold Caleb back, their hunt for horse chestnuts paused while they dropped to the carpet of pine needles. 'Booby trap,' Oliver'd whisper. 'Ten to two, turn around.' Caleb never saw the booby trap with his own eyes but always went along with West's instructions. Maybe because he had an RP accent. Everything he said sounded sophisticated and true. He'd moved back to Kent the summer before Caleb started at Tregele Comprehensive. That's when he'd met the two Joshes. Neither of them had heard of conkers. He wondered what Oliver West was doing now. He wondered if he was on Facebook.

The beat of his footsteps on the path was getting quicker. Cadence was the key to successful long-distance running. His optimal cadence was one-hundred-and-eighty strides a minute back when he was training for his first race in Ebbw Vale but it would take a few weeks to work himself back to that stage. He had to relearn it all, build strength and stamina from the ground. He was breaking a sweat, his heart opening and closing like a

RACHEL TREZISE

closed shackle padlock, *cush-cush cush-cush cush-cush*, pulse knocking against his flesh like a pinball along a chicane. There was something else as well, a prickly feeling in his legs like chicken pox on the inside. With every step the itching got worse, the taste of blood in the back of his throat. It was supposed to hurt though, wasn't it? No pain, no gain. No pressure, no diamonds. All those clichés that were true. He pushed past the horse pastures and the Scots Pine trees. Then he saw something he'd never seen before on a tract of flattened land to the side of the Kennard nursing home, a town square fashioned from wood like a cheap film set. He stopped to look properly at it. 'The fuck?' he said as he studied the model shop fronts and red telephone box. Hang on, he'd seen something on the news about this; the world was changing so quickly, people with Alzheimer's Disease didn't recognise it anymore. Dummies of old-fashioned buildings like banks and greengrocers made them feel safe again. With his carpentry skills, the old man should get a job making dementia villages for nursing homes. He could put a replica of his own carpet shop in every one. *No laminate, no rugs, no tiles, just carpets, mun!* Caleb started a jog down the ridge past the allotments Gankey had nicknamed Patagonia Gardens on account of the poor-quality soil. He gathered a bit of speed as he pounded down the hill, the soles of his trainers slapping on the gravel. He got to the footbridge that crossed over the Rhosybol River while simultaneously crossing under the railway line, a tang of engine diesel and freshwater fish mingling together, the pebble banking shrouded in a slimy skin of emerald algae.

On the other side was Trefecca. Zion Street, part of an area devastated by floods a few years back. It'd been on the national news, footage of leather armchairs and bits of a broken doll's house floating on the sludgy floodwater towards the river, Tommy Gillard hanging out of his bedroom window in his pants

104

telling the news reporters his new washing machine was full of sewage. The old man had taken it upon himself to re-carpet the five houses that didn't have insurance. 'Trust me, this is the best advertising we could ever get, Hel,' he'd said when Caleb's mother questioned him about it. 'Word of mouth is like wildfire. Nobody ever regrets being kind.' The bill came to seven grand in total. Where had that got him in the end? It's probably what wiped him out. Maybe his mother was right, maybe you had to concentrate on looking after number one these days.

The bells of St Bartholomew's clanged three times. It must have been nine o'clock. The prickling in his legs got more intense as he tried to pummel up the pavement towards the main road, the onset of a headache flaring at the base of his skull. He felt weak and nauseous. He wanted an ice cream from that van he'd seen in the street, a 99 with two flakes, crushed nuts and the raspberry sauce his old man called monkey's blood. He hadn't eaten ice cream like that since he'd taken Oscar to the van parked in the layby on Pontio Mountain last summer. He was getting giddy, a light show of neon colours playing on the screen of his mind's eye. He had to stop before he fainted. He clung to the railings of the abandoned chapel on the corner of Trip Terrace, holding himself up. He took one deep breath then another, the air cool against the roof of his mouth. In a few moments, the tingling in his legs faded. He'd been holding his breath. He realised he hadn't been breathing properly since he'd started, his blood awash with carbon dioxide instead of the oxygen his heart needed to pump. How was he going to be ready for a full triathlon if he couldn't get the basics right? He walked quickly along the main road, concentrating hard on inhaling and exhaling. As soon as he'd got into a rhythm he started to jog again. He cut over the Tynybedw bridge into the Caemawr Industrial Estate. The old man reckoned it had been jam-packed with manufacturers when he was a youngster, a steel plant that made fire extinguishers and a sewing factory that supplied Tommy Hilfiger with the silk that lined its coats. He swore the concrete-filled tank in front of the abandoned gatehouse had been an ornamental pond teeming with a rare variety of Koi Carp. Now it was Zodiac Windows and a handful of derelict zinc-roofed warehouses where smackheads went to jack up. Rushed graffiti across the entrance gate of the old Christmas trimming factory said, 'CHED EVANS = FAKE NEWS.'

He was going great guns now, breathing steady. Endorphins were releasing along the length of his spine, the tension sucking his guts taut vanished. The estate gave way to a tree-lined path running the length of the rugby pitch and a reek of warm dog shit, the waste bin overflowing with plastic parcels of excrement, little red or black bags tied with double knots. Matteo Spinetti was folding the visor back on the Pegasus café as Caleb rounded the corner into Tregele. It was the last Italian café left in the town, windows crammed with dusty jars of Army & Navies and Sherbert Lemons.

'Running, are you?' Matteo said, watching him dart past.

'Aye.'

'Right you are,' Matteo said.

The Italians had been here forever, Caleb thought. Why were the Italians OK but not the Poles? A heavily-tattooed bloke in a Superdry T-shirt was leant in the portal to the gully, a massive electronic cigarette in his hand. Caleb would have gone that way if the bloke hadn't been there, out of sight of the prying eyes on the high street. But the shops were closed now, anyway. There wouldn't be many people about. The burnt sugar smell of the e-cigarette turned to a stench of scorched mutton as Caleb ran past the traffic lights, the kebab shop and old boarded-up bank falling back into the distance.

'Jenkins!' From the corner of his eye Caleb could see the tables set up outside the Centaur, enveloped by a scrubby artificial hedge. Men with their pint glasses tilted to their mouths on one side, women with their spidery false eyelashes on the other. He'd forgotten about the beer garden. 'Oi! Jenkins!' He didn't want to have a conversation about his father's business going kaput or what Savannah Sayer had done. He didn't want to talk about anything to anyone, let alone Aaron Kinsey, one of Mason's ganja-smoking mates. He pretended not to hear, his eyes scanning the paving slabs below like the secrets of the universe were engraved on them. 'Jenkins, mun!' Kinsey, called one more time. Caleb kept his sprint up past the chemist, heart beating like a kick drum.

The purple UKIP sticker in the phone shop window said, 'Let's Take Our Country Back'. Back to what? Caleb wondered. All that stuff like corporal and capital punishment, orphanages and workhouses and infant mortality they showed on 'Who Do You Think You Are?' all the time. When his mother had cared about rumours, there was one going around that the owner of the phone shop was listed on the sex offenders' register. 'I'm going to bring it up at the next Chamber of Trade AGM,' she'd said not knowing she would have lost her own shop by then. Maybe the phone shop owner wanted to take the country back to before the sex offenders' register existed, to a time when the age of consent was twelve years old.

When he finally looked up, Caleb saw a cluster of middle-aged women gathered on the pavement outside the old carpet shop, the sleeves of their pastel-coloured blazers rolled to their elbows, bare limbs crisscrossed with purple zig-zag veins. They were holding dainty glasses of fizzy wine in their hands, chattering on about the referendum in Welsh. 'Y prif weinidog hwn! Dim blydi ceilliau.' Something about David Cameron's balls.

'Esgusodwch fi,' Caleb said with his best school Welsh as he cut a path through the women. Only then did he notice the plate-glass windows in the old shop, bedecked with gold calligraphy, bunting strung all around. Amazing Glazing wasn't a glazier; it was a bakery, its walls covered with pink wallpaper. Framed prints of flamingos wearing diamond tiaras or chunky white tennis shoes. His mother's hinged counter was gone, replaced with a glass display loaded with cakes and garlands of plastic roses. Caleb froze. 'The fuck?' he said, coming to a stop. The old women turned to glare at him, the heels of their shoes scraping on the pavement. 'Ofnadwy!' one of them said.

A woman with a heap of cherry-red hair popped up from behind the glass display, a bottle of wine in her hand. Perfectly spherical tits like a pair of honeydew melons squashed in a tank top under her denim dungarees. 'Caleb boy!' she said beckoning him inside. It was Sioned Treasure, a girl he'd known distantly at school. He'd liked the look of her in their registration classes but that was the only time he did see her – she was in the top sets for drama and languages. Then she'd got straight out of Rhosybol like all the cleverest people did. Caleb stepped cautiously into the shop. The Victorian floor tiles had been pressure-washed and polished, the lattice pattern gleaming, a hairline crack along the border sealed with epoxy resin. 'Sioned, girl,' he said, becoming aware of the meaty BO smell under his arms. He raised his right elbow and sniffed at the hot stink of his pit. Sioned winced. 'Running,' he said, shrugging defensively.

She put down the bottle and handed him a cake. Yellow icing studded with chocolate buttons. 'Oh,' he said. 'Ta.'

'How's it going anyway? I heard about the Iron Man stuff. My

Nanna sent me all her old copies of the *Rhosybol Herald*. She doesn't understand it's all online.'

'I was on the telly too,' Caleb said, his voice brimming with hubris.

'*Made in Wales*?' Sioned said, one eyebrow raised. 'I saw the *first* one. So exploitative!'

Caleb's blood soured. *He* could rubbish it if he liked. Not her. What did *she* know?

'No offense,' she said, registering the sting on his face. She picked a bunch of keys off the counter and weighed them in her hand. 'I'd better lock up. We open officially in the morning. I've got to get this mess cleared.' She emerged from behind the display and tried to guide him to the door, hand pressed to the small of his back. 'Thanks for popping in, Cal. It's lovely to see you.'

'So what's this all about?' he said inspecting the bubblegum-pink walls, standing his ground. 'I thought you were too good for Rhosybol. I thought you were gone.'

'Cakes, Cal! I've always loved baking! You know that. I always made the cakes for the school Twmpath. I studied dance at Roehampton but these days the jobs are few and far between. It's competitive. And I'm older. My body's changing.' She waved stiffly at her waist, glancing self-consciously at him before gazing off. 'You look alright to me,' he said.

Sioned giggled. 'Anyway, this place was going for a song.'

'Because it was repossessed. It was my old man's place. The carpet shop. Remember?'

Sioned recoiled. 'No, I didn't realise.'

'It's been tough on my old man. They lost the house in Ninian Close. They're living with *me* if you can believe that. And they say kids can't leave home now until their early thirties.'

'Oh God, I'm sorry,' she said, her voice sugar-coated like the woman on the phone at the DVLA. 'You could get somewhere else though, couldn't you? The rent's cheap in Trebermawr.'

'Yeah,' Caleb said. Couldn't she see he wanted *this* shop? He wanted his old life. He wanted everything back to normal. Now his little pipe dream was wrecked because of her. He looked at the Live/Laugh/Love plaque on the wall behind the till. Everything was pastel and glittery like a heap of unicorn vomit. 'I saw lots of properties before I found this place,' Sioned said. 'I could help you find something. Pop in some time for a cuppa. I've got a list of local premises coming up for rent. Goronwy Lewis gave it to me.'

Caleb eyed her uncertainly. Could that be it? Could he get a new place, a blank sheet, unsullied by his father's failure? 'Thanks for the fairy cake.' He held it up like a drink to toast her.

Sioned rolled her eyes. '*Cup*cake!' she said. 'They're called cupcakes now. Anyone would think you grew up in the seventies or something.' Caleb laughed. He may as well have, his old man playing punk music and prattling on about old Labour his whole childhood. He *felt* twenty years older than he actually was. 'Alright,' he said. He spat it out: 'Cupcake! There!'

Sioned smiled, porcelain skin pale against her slew of blazing hair. 'Didn't kill you, did it?'

He folded the pleated paper case back on the sponge and forced it, whole, into his mouth, the sugar paste fizzing against his palate. 'What d'you reckon?' she said watching him chew. 'Sweet,' he said. He handed her the empty case. He wiped his mouth on his wrist and stomped out of the old shop, cortisone pouring into his bloodstream as he cut through the Welsh-speaking women. 'See you, Cal,' she shouted after him.

A Citroen Saxo careered down the road in a metallic-blue blur, horn squealing at the drinkers in front of the Centaur, who whooped and cheered back at it. Caleb reeled to the end of the block and escaped down Queensferry Street, a surge of flat-out panic filling his chest until it hurt. Part of the cake was lodged in his throat. He sat down in the bricked-up doorway at the back of the barber shop, light from the foyer of the assisted-living flats opposite reflected in a pool of yellow at his feet. He drew the crumbs up out of his gullet with a plug of olive phlegm and spat it into the kerb. There was an empty condom packet in the gutter, Durex Real Feel. Did anyone use condoms anymore? You never saw them in porn videos. What would his life be like now if he'd had one on him that first night in Trebermawr? Savannah couldn't have made up that story about Oscar but he guessed she'd have made one up about something else. '*Tell me lies, tell me sweet little lies,*' he sang sarcastically to himself.

Next to the condom were a couple of small silver canisters. Nitrous Oxide. 'Hippy crack,' Mason called it. Apparently, the millennials couldn't get enough of them. Caleb couldn't understand why, all it did was make you laugh. 'Live laugh love'. It must have been about quarter to ten, almost dark. It didn't go completely dark in early summer in Rhosybol. The stars were too bright. Instead, the sky changed from a light blue to a deep purple colour. It was lilac now, smoke-grey at the edge of the bowl. A pipistrelle flew out of a crevice in the roof of the flats.

Caleb stood up. The frantic feeling in his chest had faded, replaced with an oncoming fatigue. He started dawdling along, legs like ton weights. He could get back to Iscoed Street via Mutton Tump, an isolated footpath that cut across the edge of Cwmyoy Mountain, without going back down the high street. He followed the babble of the river along the spinal column of the town until he got to the steep iron railway bridge hidden behind the entrance to Penyrenglyn Industrial Estate. The bridge seemed to tremble under his footsteps as he took the treads two at a time. His old man reckoned it used to be a popular spot for suicides, but Caleb hadn't heard of anyone killing themselves since all those hangings in the Gwaun Valley ten years ago. It had been the news of the world for a while, photographs of dead teenagers on the cover of every newspaper on the Siddiqui's shelves. Then a sudden media blackout, as if the story itself had died.

At least he still had his job. He'd have to grovel in the morning, agree to whatever Morris wanted. Smile and apologise for going outside in his PPE. No sir, yes sir. Cleflock had him by the gonads, a frog in a pot of slowly boiling water, slave to the corporate machine. But they had to give him a warning before they sacked him. He was sure he'd read that in the handbook. And he was a good butcher. He still had his job at least. And he could keep trying to save some money. He could look at Sioned's list.

On the other side of the railway bridge, he set off running up Mutton Tump, the sudden movement generating an unanticipated rush of restless energy. The smell of sap filled his nose as he pounded up the footpath, wild Welsh heart beating out of his chest, the lights of Tregele getting further away. A few minutes ahead, he could see the outline of the kissing gate appear. He stopped in front of it and pressed it open, the metal cold to the touch, its hinges creaking dramatically. He checked the tracking app on his phone. Sixty minutes of substandard on/off activity had tapered into an awesome two-minute half-mile, the green line on the graph soaring up like a rocket. That was the quickest he'd ever recorded. All he needed to do was stretch the pace out across 5km and the triathlon wasn't lost. If he ran again tomorrow and everyday next week, he could maybe still scrape a win.

Back in his own neighbourhood now, Council Christine's Range Rover Vogue was parked in front of his Puma, the tacky foam ladybird stuck on its aerial making it look like a remote-control toy. The street light was shining on the Polling Station banner stuck to the gate of the bowling club. That must have been where people around here went to vote. He'd passed it twice in the car but on his way out for his run he'd jogged in the opposite direction. In Ninian Close, Siloh Chapel had always been their local polling station. He remembered how proud he'd been of himself after voting in the general elections of 2010 and 2015; a real grown-up with real responsibilities. Gankey Jenkins had told him once how important it was to use his vote: 'People like us didn't get a say until 1867! That's only a century ago, mind, bach.'

Then his old man had come into the room. 'You know he's too young for all that, Dad. Ten years old, he is.'

'Aye, well there's that,' Gankey had said, winking at Caleb.

As he got closer to the Iscoed Street junction, he saw a figure in the bowling club window waving frantically at him. He started down the path towards the clubhouse to get a tidy look. Council Christine.

'It's you,' he said when she appeared in the doorway, adjusting a fringed pashmina around her sunburned shoulders. 'I saw your car. I thought you were in the house with Mammy.'

'Doing my bit for democracy,' she said. 'I thought you were the presiding officer coming to collect the ballot box. He has to officially seal it before we can start clearing up.' She gestured at a man in his late thirties sitting behind a wallpapering table in front of the shuttered bar. She was the kind of person who'd patronise Sioned's cake shop, Caleb thought. She'd be up there tomorrow ordering a vegan-friendly Red Velvet with chocolate hundreds-and-thousands. Then she'd put a photograph of it up on Facebook. 'Have you voted?' she said.

'Nah, I lost my polling card.' It must have been on the cupboard with the reminder for the car tax. 'You don't need that,' she said. She looked back at the Roman numerals on the wall clock. The long hand was a few seconds away from the XII at the top. 'Quick,' she said beckoning him inside. She shuffled back to the wallpapering table and ripped a voting slip from a booklet. 'Jenkins: Caleb,' she said to the man in front of the bar, who ran an aluminium straightedge down a long list of names printed on a sheet of A1. 'Got it,' he said, crossing a line through one of them. Christine steered Caleb to a wooden cubicle erected in the middle of the tiny dance floor.

He found himself hunched over the shelf inside, considering the words printed on the slip. 'Remain' meant that everything would stay the same but 'Leave' meant something had to change. So what if everything went tits-up for a few months? No pain, no gain. No pressure, no diamonds. It was as if the world had frozen like an overloaded IT system, so many pages simultaneously open that nobody really knew what was going on. Even his brother, who had at least five GCSEs, thought the contrails from aeroplanes emitted biological agents. Someone needed to knock it all off and back on again. It was like his old man always used to say about the temperamental till in the carpet shop: when in doubt give it a clout.

A car pulled up outside. 'Quick, Cal,' Christine said. 'The officer's here.'

He picked up the chewed pencil attached with dirty string to the cubicle and quickly scratched a graphite cross into the space. He folded the slip in half and dropped it into the ballot box, the man behind the table grinning madly at him. 'There you are, love,' Christine said, guiding him back to the sliding door. He was on his way to the Iscoed Street junction when the front door of the Unicorn opened with a bang. An old long-haired hippy stepped into the street, a cigarette held up to his whiskery chops. The flint of his lighter sparked blue but failed to ignite. He plucked the fag from his lips and sang a line of the song playing on the karaoke machine inside: '*Hey bay–bee! There ain't no easy way out—*'

'Night, pal,' Caleb shouted as he headed up and across the road.

He was three yards away from the house when he felt something fleshy clap against his face. He couldn't see anything, his nostrils filled with a sharp, rusty smell. 'Guess,' someone said, a hot breath on his neck. Caleb's body stiffened. He hadn't heard any footsteps. 'Guess,' the voice said again, thick and slow.

'Mason?'

'Ad 'ew then, butt.' Mason dropped his hands, clasping them loosely around Caleb's throat.

'Dickhead,' Caleb said, rolling his shoulders, his brother's grip thrown off.

'Got a favour to ask,' Mason said, the whites of eyes shining under the streetlight.

'What now?' Caleb said.

'I wouldn't ask if I wasn't desperate, bro.'

'What?'

'The agency's got me an overnighter in Temple Green. I need to borrow the car.'

Caleb laughed. 'Fuck off, you header. How'm I s'posed to get to work in the morning?'

'Iss only 'leven til four. I'll be back before you're up.'

'Five hours' work? What's the point?'

'They'll take me off the books if I don't do it. That's what it's like with these agency twats, butt. They give you a couple of awkward shifts to test your loyalty. If you can get through that they'll take you on. You know what it's like. We're working-class, bro. We're easy meat.'

'No can do, Mase. I've got my own shit going on at Cleflock. They've called me into the office first thing in the morning. My supervisor's been waiting for an excuse to get rid of me since the day I started, jobsworth bastard.'

'Come on, Cal. I'll be home by five. Risk it for a biscuit, bro. I'll be back in time, I promise.'

Caleb shook his head. 'No way, José.'

'Thanks a lot, bro. Very supportive of you, as per.'

'Fuck up, Mase,' Caleb said. He wasn't in the mood for emotional blackmail.

Mason turned back to peer at the pub, face solemn-looking. As he pivoted around to face the street again, he punched Caleb hard in the ribs, his body forced toward the cars at the kerb. Caleb pressed his hand to his tit, dazed by the unexpected violence.

'The fuck?' he said as he swung for Mason. He landed a weak uppercut on the side of his skull. Mason staggered but came back at him, nostrils flared, face purple with rage. He charged into Caleb, flipping him over like a pancake in a frying pan. The ground smelt like three different kinds of piss. Caleb grabbed at Mason's ankles and pulled him down to his level. They rolled a few times across the cool concrete pavement, panting like asthmatic mouth-breathers. They came to a stationary jumble of arms and legs next to the iron drain in the gutter. Mason climbed up onto his knees and slapped himself on the midriff.

'Come on 'en, Triathlon Man.' He tapped his solar plexus, inviting Caleb to strike. 'Come at me, bro!'

Caleb launched himself at his brother, arms thrown around his torso, right bicep wedged against the side of his neck. With the whole weight of his shoulder, he forced Mason's chin down to his collarbone. He kept him in a chokehold, Mason struggling to breathe through his nose. When he kicked out, Caleb reduced the pressure, just enough to let him speak. 'Submit,' he said like he used to when they'd wrestled as kids.

'It's alright for you,' said Mason, voice strangled. 'You've *got* a job.'

Caleb let go of him.

Mason scooted away, a crab scuttling across hot sand. 'Arsehole,' he said.

Caleb leaned back on his elbows to look at the summer triangle constellation overhead.

Mason pulled a half-smoked zoot from his jacket pocket and smoothed out its creased paper. 'Ghost Train,' he said. 'Fucking peng.'

'Look at you,' Caleb said to him. 'You can't go ten minutes without a smoke. How could you hold down a job?'

Mason lit the joint. 'Easy. It's standing on an assembly line in a nail-polish factory, not rocket surgery.' He took a drag then blew the smoke in Caleb's direction. 'Do you even know how fucking humiliating it is for me to have to beg you for a lend of the car for five hours sticking stickers on bottles of nail polish?'

Caleb thought about Morris calling him a numpty in front of everyone. 'Yeah,' he said.

'No, you don't. You've *got* a job. You've got the house. You're the big hero who saved the day when Mammy and Daddy lost the shop. She worships the ground *you* walk on.' He offered the spliff to Caleb. Caleb shook his head. 'I'm the big disappointment. Inferior second child.'

'You don't make it easy on yourself, Mase. Like, the earth isn't flat, for fuck's sake.'

Mason was silent for a few moments. 'It is, Cal. I know it is. That's the only thing I know for sure. Everything else is pure chaos. I wish I *didn't* know, butt.'

Jesus Christ. Why couldn't he get his head around the fact conspiracy theorists were part of a conspiracy to use stupid people to spread disinformation? 'Why?' Caleb said, bracing himself.

'Because the truth is hard. The truth is lonely. It's fucking demoralising, bro. You find out one thing then another then another then another until you realise …' He looked up at Caleb, eyes narrow and rheumy. 'You've got to believe in s*omething*.'

Caleb shook his head.

'So can I borrow the car tonight or what? Come on, bro. I've got to be there by 'leven. You're the one who wants me to get a job. You can sleep in the bed.'

'I don't want to sleep in the bed 'til it's changed. I don't fancy catching your pubic lice.' But he did. He wanted to sleep, just for once, on a full-size mattress on a real bed frame and stretch all four of his limbs out at the same time; starfish like a king.

He stood and marched up the street towards the house, Mason dawdling behind. He took the Yale key from his shorts pocket and opened the front door. The television was on in the living room, the volume turned up so loud he could hear the presenter through the wall: 'Good evening and welcome to the end of a momentous day.' Dramatic orchestral music in the background. He scooped the car keys out of the wooden bowl on the cupboard and handed them to Mason, who'd stayed on the doorstep. 'You'll need to put some petrol in. Call it a tenner.'

Mason nodded.

'Be careful,' Caleb said. 'There was an accident in Hebron this morning, nasty too.'

'Yes, Dad,' Mason said, saluting him. He walked to the driver's side of the car.

'Home by five,' Caleb warned him.

'I promised, didn't I?' Mason said.

Council Christine was coming up the street, kitten heels tap-tapping on the pavement. Caleb pulled the front door closed. 'We'll be here until dawn, watching the votes come in,' the TV presenter said through the wall. 'Blue for leave. Yellow for remain. Could it really be *this* close?'

The bathroom was still steamy from his mother's evening bath, her rings left in the soap dish. Caleb eyed the names of the old man's antidepressant medications lined across the shelf above the sink as he peeled his shorts down his legs and threw them into the washing basket. Cipralex, Zoloft, Flurazepam.

He stepped into the tub and unfolded the concertina screen. He turned the shower lever as far as it would go, the stream of lukewarm water washing his dried sweat down his chest and belly. He rubbed the water, colder by the zeptosecond, into his eyelashes and ear canals, making sure any blood left from the slaughterhouse was gone. He'd have to look his best for that meeting in the office in the morning. When he'd finished, he folded the screen back and stepped out of the bath. The balls of his feet smacked on the ceramic tiles as he made, bollock-naked, for the landing, too tired to properly dry off.

He threw the duvet back on the bed and sat down, the undersheet a mix of his mother's fabric conditioner and the parmesan whiff of his brother's feet. He checked the time on the screen of his phone. It was only ten thirty-seven. It felt like the middle of the night. A train pulled out of Tregele Station, the clack of its wheels echoing through the drainage channel under the Iscoed Street pavement. He lay down, legs extended, toes pointed up like a ballet dancer. Then he let go of the stretch, the small of his back sinking into the mattress. A dog barked on Mutton Tump. A couple left the Unicorn, his 'n' hers' laughter reverberating, loud at first, then trailing off. A car raced over the Sychpant, tyres thumping on the cattle grid.

He stared across at the empty bed settee, an indistinct lump against the plum-coloured sky. He could see the white glow of the moon through the thin Spiderman curtains. Or was that next door's security light? This was where Oscar used to sleep, in a car-shaped bed with a camouflage-print duvet cover and a soft Minion toy Caleb had won for him on a Barry Island claw machine. He forced himself to think instead of the graceful architecture of Sioned Treasure's tits. Of the girl from payroll in the canteen at break time. Had she really looked at him like she wanted to eat him alive or had he been tripping off that early morning toke on his brother's weed? She was right in front of him, her dirty plate in her hands, light from the window reflecting in her glossy brown hair. Then he was back at his rail with the carcasses, as if he'd imagined it all. His heart jumped into his throat at the thought of the factory, adrenaline flooding into his bloodstream. What the fuck was he going to do if his brother wasn't back in time with the car? There wasn't a train or a bus that could get him from Tregele to Derwen Uchaf at that time in the morning. He'd have to cycle. He remembered his front tyre had a puncture. He imagined himself rifling through the metal compartments of his old man's toolbox for the repair kit. But he hadn't seen his dad's toolbox since his parents had moved to Iscoed Street. Had his old man sold it as part of the bankruptcy deal with the bank? Where was it? Next thing he saw himself running on a broken boardwalk, scorching sun burning the nape of his neck. He was wearing a red baseball cap, long socks pulled up to his knees. He could smell the sea: saltmarsh and algae. A seagull cawed. 'Shrimp kebab,' someone said in an American accent. 'Shrimp creole, shrimp gumbo. Shrimp is the fruit of the sea!' He was dreaming Forrest Gump. The fishy smell slowly turned to the raw, elemental stink of Cleflock Beef. He remembered he was in Mason's bed, the duvet stuck with cold sweat to his stomach.

He lay still until he'd caught his breath, his heart rate gradually decreasing. Nothing. Finally, sleep was overcoming him. Then he jerked suddenly, violently, a sensation like falling from a great height. He threw the duvet off his chest and turned over, the undersheet cool against his clammy skin. He pressed his cheekbone to the musty pillow, his arm crossed over the empty space next to him. As he fell asleep, he felt a pang of contentment vibrate in his belly like a plucked guitar string – a vague sense of something brilliant having happened, though he couldn't quite remember what it was.

ACKNOWLEDGEMENTS

'*All over people changing their votes / Along with their overcoats / If Adolf Hitler flew in today / They'd send a limousine anyway*' from '(White Man) In Hammersmith Palais' by The Clash (Joe Strummer/Mick Jones, 1978)

'*Tell me lies, tell me sweet little lies*' from 'Little Lies' by Fleetwood Mac (Christine McVie/Eddy Quintela, 1987)

'*Hey baby, there ain't no easy way out*' from 'I Won't Back Down' by Tom Petty (Tom Petty/Jeff Lynne, 1989)

With thanks to Gwen Davies, David Prince, Rhiannon White and Evie Manning at Common Wealth Theatre, Michael Sheen, and all at Parthian.

PARTHIAN   Journeys

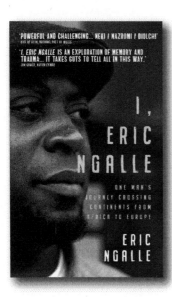

I, ERIC NGALLE:
One Man's Journey Crossing Continents from Africa to Europe

ERIC NGALLE

ISBN 978-1-912109-10-4
£9.99 • Paperback

'Powerful and challenging...
neki / nazromi / diolch!'
**– Ifor ap Glyn,
National Poet of Wales**

JUST SO YOU KNOW:
Essays of Experience

EDITED BY HANAN ISSA, DURRE
SHAHWAR & ÖZGÜR UYANIK

ISBN 978-1-912681-82-2
£9.00 • Paperback

'Smart, bold and fresh – these are
voices we need to hear'
**– Darren Chetty, author, and
contributor of** *The Good Immigrant*

'This probing, honest and
illuminating collection of essays is of
course very timely but it's also one
of the best books published in Wales
in many a moon.'
– Jon Gower, Nation.Cymru

PARTHIAN

Fiction

FRESH APPLES
RACHEL TREZISE

ISBN 978-1-913640-26-2

£8.99 • Paperback

**Winner of the EDS
Dylan Thomas Prize**

'Laugh-out-loud funny.' **– Peter
Florence,** *Harpers and Queen*

'A totally original voice... can be
easily compared to James Joyce's
Dubliners.' **– Andrew Davies**

'A major new literary talent.'
– Mario Basini

WORK, SEX
& RUGBY
LEWIS DAVIES

ISBN 978-1-913640-23-1

£8.99 • Paperback

**Winner of the World Book Day
Award for Wales**

'Riotously Funny' **–** *Western Mail*

'Grimly realistic' **–** *gwales.com*

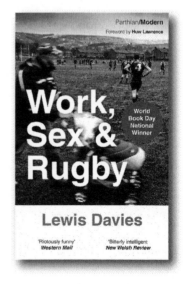